MW01128583

In The Forest Of
The Night

Tyger! tyger! burning bright
In the forests of the night,
What immortal hand or eye
Could frame thy fearful symmetry?

In The Forest Of The Night

Larry Ellis

Writers Club Press

San Jose   New York   Lincoln   Shanghai

In The Forest Of The Night

All Rights Reserved © 2001 by Larry R. Ellis

No part of this book may be reproduced or transmitted in any form or by any means, graphic, electronic, or mechanical, including photocopying, recording, taping, or by any information storage retrieval system, without the permission in writing from the publisher.

Writers Club Press
an imprint of iUniverse, Inc.

For information address:
iUniverse, Inc.
5220 S. 16th St., Suite 200
Lincoln, NE 68512
www.iuniverse.com

This novel is a work of fiction. Names, characters, places and events are either the product of the author's imagination or are used fictitiously. Any resemblance to actual occurences, places or people, living or dead, is completely coincidental.

ISBN: 0-595-19500-8

Printed in the United States of America

This book is dedicated to the memory of my grandfather, Robert Lee Ellis, 1888–1982, a soldier, miner, and union man.

Foreword

And there was a certain man of Zorah, of the family of the Danites, whose name was Manoah; and his wife was barren, and bare not. And the angel of the LORD appeared unto the woman, and said to her, Behold now, thou art barren, and bearest not: but thou shalt conceive, and bear a son. Now therefore beware, I pray thee, and drink not wine nor strong drink, and eat not any unclean thing: For, lo, thou shalt conceive, and bear a son; and no razor shall come on his head: for the child shall be a Nazarite unto God from the womb: and he shall begin to deliver Israel out of the hand of the Philistines.

And the woman bare a son, and called his name Samson: and the child grew, and the LORD blessed him.

Judges 13:2-5, 24

Preface

The sheriff's car topped the hill and came down the narrow blacktop road through the great and wilting oaks. It had rained a little that morning and wisps of steam rose from the hot black pavement in the unshaded places. The car moved very swiftly, quietly, as if with a sure knowledge that there could be no opposing traffic, that the single lane was clear around every blind turn. As if with the knowledge that its unenvied purpose was immutable. The car slowed quickly, without sound, and pulled right off the road and onto a short, broad clearing, a wedge of weeds, vines and unkempt grass at the dull point of which, back against the forest, sat a house trailer.

The front door of the trailer stood open. The storm door was aluminum with a top pane of glass that had been shattered. It opened out over a small metal stoop, now at a near perfect ninety-degree angle to the front wall of the trailer, perfectly motionless, as if rusted or frozen. The inner door was opened in, the mirror image of the outside door.

The deputy left the engine idling and the door of the cruiser open. All sound was dampened in the soggy heat. The deputy walked toward the open door. He was a large man and in full uniform, ranger's hat and gunbelt. He did not draw his gun.

John, you in there?

He stepped onto the metal stoop and saw a lamp burning inside the front room.

John Helton?

He started through the doorway, but then saw the body on the carpet, face up, blood dried on the face and where it had flowed onto the carpet from the ruptured forehead to the body's left. The deputy stepped back out of the doorway and drew his gun, looked right and left and backed away from the trailer and to the cruiser. He laid his revolver on the seat beside him and backed the cruiser onto the road and drove back to the edge of the clearing and pulled back off the road and there turned the cruiser around so it again faced the trailer which was visible to him now through a line of trees. He let the engine idle as he made contact with the county dispatcher and he waited there, with the trailer in his sight, until backup arrived.

That afternoon, as he and another deputy took inventory of the mare's nest of a master bedroom in the trailer, the other deputy spoke.

You know what. This case ain't ever gonna
be solved. You know why? The damn companies don't want it solved. If this ain't the

damn company's doin' I don't know what is. They ain't never liked Helton anyway. He ain't got no family and was too stupid to give a shit about anything and the companies couldn't control him. They didn't have no way of gettin' to him. The companies think—you mark my words—the companies think Helton was in on that far that was set to the guard shack on the picket line up at Sharples. Killed that guard. And you know what? Helton probably was. He was the only one that still had any damn balls. You know what? This damn department won't ever solve this case because they own us, too. The damn companies own us. I'll deny I ever said it.

He slid open the door of the bedroom closet and looked down onto six metal boxes, each with a six-digit tattoo and a slot in the top.

Acknowledgements

Thanks to Betty MacQueen, Helen Carper, Mary Liming, Douglas Preston, Rudy DiTrapano, Miller Bushong and Anna Crawford for their help and encouragement.

PART ONE

I

The car was jacked up high at the right front tire, its grill a chrome mouth slanting up at the corner like a sneer. Jack Sampson was facing the car and wiping his hands on a rag. He was exactly six feet tall.

He watched the boy try to lower the jack. The boy was young and skinny with blue jeans and no shirt. He had sweated and dried, the day's dirt in contoured streaks faint on his suntanned skin, the markings of a wild animal.

The boy slid the straight end of the tire tool—a rod in the shape of a relaxed L—into a fitting protruding from the collar at the top of the jack. The rod slanted down, the lug wrench end seeming to droop.

The boy grasped the lever with both hands. His arms were extended and locked and he slid his left foot back and leaned his weight against the lever. The lever did not move and he continued to press, his face flushed, his arms finally quivering. "It ain't no use," he grunted. "Thing must be broke." He continued to strain.

Sampson moved around the jacked-up corner of the car and waved the boy off. "Let me see."

The boy stepped back. "There ain't no way," he said.

Sampson likewise took the lever in both hands and leaned over the lever and pushed against it. He held the press for a moment. The lever began a very slow descent and metal whined with strain until the boy, now wide-eyed, spoke. "Stop, Jack. You're breakin' it." He pointed to the jack.

Sampson relaxed and ran his finger around the outside of the fitting that held the tire tool in the jack. At the bottom of the cylinder the intestine-like bulge of the weld; beside that, the sharp points and new edges of the splitting metal. He stood for a moment and looked the car end to end. The stick-on letters on the driver's door "Bandy Police," the decal of the policeman's shield. He nodded his head, wiped his hands on his uniform pants, and slipped the tire tool out of the collar and set it on the concrete floor. He wrapped one hand around the stem of the jack just under the black collar. He looked at the boy. "You hold this thing right here, and when I get the car up, you jerk it out. Do it in a hurry."

"You cain't do that. Nobody could do that."

"I reckon I'll need to get other help then."

"I'll do it," said the boy. He stepped to the jack and went to his knees, as far away as he could get and still reach, and he took the jack in one hand as he had been shown. He turned his head away from the car.

Sampson reached under the high corner of the car with both hands and felt

for grips. Then he bent at the knees and waist, his chest against the quarter-panel, elbows and forearms pressed against his thighs. His badge clicked against the car. "I don't want to have to do this twice," he said. He scooted one foot and then another back away from the car. "You ready?"

"This is crazy," said the boy.

"You just get it done. It'll be all right. You ready?"

"Yeah."

Sampson pushed his body against the car with the upward slant. The car tilted higher now and the jack rose from the floor. The boy, looking in fear, yanked the jack clanging onto the floor and covered his head with his hands. Sampson jerked away from the car and it dropped, the new tire mashing against the floor, the car rocking with the high squeaks and low groans of straining metal, as if momentarily alive.

"Damn," said the boy.

Sampson picked up the jack and tried the collar. Now it moved with the flick of his finger. "Look at that."

He leaned the jack against the wall, picked up the tire iron, knelt by the new tire and began tightening by a half turn each of the lug nuts on the repaired wheel.

"How strong are you?" the boy asked.

"I don't know."

"We gonna go patrol now?"

"No."

"I could go with you. I know where some boys has been stealing from the mines."

"What are they stealing?"

"Mining cable."

"How much?"

"Hundred foot."

"From over at Drawdy?"

"Yeah. I think."

"Why would somebody steal something like that?"

"I don't know. Some of them boys just thinks it's fun, I guess."

"Bobby Graley in on it?"

The boy frowned. "I don't know. I don't think he was."

"Who's buying mining cable?"

"I don't know."

Sampson set the hubcap in place over the lugnuts, drew back, and rammed the open heel of his other hand against the center of the metal disk. Then he stood up and looked down at the boy.

"You tell me right now where that mining cable is."

"Shit, man. I don't know. I wasn't in on it."

"You tell me where it'll be tomorrow, then."

"I don't know. Probably in the river somewhere."

"Over by Sand Falls?"

"Yeah. Probably be around in there somewhere," the boy nodded.

"In that hole below the fast water?"

"That's where I'd look," he still nodded.

"If it ain't there tomorrow, I'm gonna have some other questions."

"I know it. Let's go on patrol. There's no telling what might be going on out there."

Sampson took keys from his pocket and opened the trunk of the car and dropped the jack and tire tool into the trunk. He did not look at the boy. "I'm not patrollin' tonight." He shut the trunk. "It's going to get dark."

"Hell, it gets dark ever night."

Sampson took a rag from his back pocket and wiped at the grease marks on the trunk lid.

"You ought not be talking that way."

The boy froze, fixed on Sampson. "I know it," he said.

"You get on home."

The boy started out the garage doorway, then turned back to Sampson. "I want a grape pop. I helped you."

Sampson tossed the rag onto a shelf and pulled the hanging chain to kill the light. He started to the doorway and into the late afternoon sunlight. He dusted one hand against the other. "All right," he said. "We'll have us a can of pop."

2

*She remembered the skinny repairman, his expressionless,
death-like face in the yellow and purple lights of the jukebox. A fist of keys dangling from his slack belt, greasy
hair hanging from his forehead as he dipped his face
down, arms extended into the opened top of the machine.
Those first years he would bring with him a short stack of
new 45s. The mines were all working then and his visits
were regular, the new records symbols of sophistication in
their glossy commercial sleeves. He would unlock the top
front of the machine, flip a switch inside, then scan the
chart on the front of the machine, stopping, punching a
letter and a number, letter and a number.*

*The machine would click like a ratchet wrench as the
stream of 45s rounded the top, emerging then submerg-
ing like targets at a carnival shooting gallery. When the
clicking and movement stopped, the selected record for a
moment the stationary eyeball of a neon Cyclops, the
man would pluck the 45 from its brace with one hand
and drop in its replacement with the other all before the
brace made its downward turn to the spinning turntable.*

*His later visits were strictly repair calls. As the
machine aged, certain selections would from time to
time not lower onto the turntable. The chosen record*

would surface, begin to tilt forward, then freeze, then a low hum from the machine and all stopped.

Then he came with no new records, only an elongated plier-like tool and a can of spray lubricant. He hurried now and cursed more frequently. Whatever he did to the inside of the machine, she did not see.

"You ought to get you a CD machine. They ain't nobody even makin' these little records anymore." He said this to Gene, her husband.

"Cost you a thousand dollars deposit. I'll bring you in a poker machine, too. One that pays off. You'll get your thousand dollars back in a couple months."

She was having none of that. Gambling was gambling, however you did it. This was a family restaurant, and what business did a poker machine have in the same room with a picture of the Lord Jesus Christ, she asked her husband. Which did he think was the most important, anyway?

Now the repairman did not come at all. He was almost two years into a five-year sentence for bribing the sheriff for protection of his poker machines, which had been operating, to the chagrin of the IRS, in nearly every other public place in the county. The repairman had turned state's evidence and testified against the sheriff and chief deputy who were now doing ten and eight years, respectively.

The good side of it was that, since nobody wanted to be identified with any machine the repairman had operated, Gene and Betty no longer had to pay any rent on the jukebox. The bad thing was that nobody else knew how to fix it and nowadays when a selection would refuse to drop onto the turntable, she would just cover over its place on the selection chart with black tape and settle for a little less variety.

By now there was a whole lot less variety. There were only twelve selections left that worked and, because she did know how to change the records around, all twelve of those were Ferlin Husky records. She kept the inside switch flipped all the time so the thing would play without quarters.

So there it sat, an adopted orphan, its back covering a rectangle of green paint three coats older than the rest of the room, its squatty legs mashing nickel-sized circles into the linoleum. Bulky, gaudy, and ethnically pure, it was an obstacle to anyone trying to reach the back table in the back room at Gene's Home Style Food and the only charitably-funded outlet for the performing arts in Boone County, West Virginia.

THERE WERE only four people in the back room tonight. They were all men and all seated at one table. The two lamps in the room were old household furniture. Unmatched, and at opposite ends of the room, they gave divergent shadows to everything in it: tables, chairs, and men. The lamplight was insufficient and yellow-grey and held, like mist holds a rainbow, the dim carnival halo of the jukebox. Three of the men wore uniforms: one blue-shirted city cop, one black-shirted deputy sheriff, one green-shirted state trooper. The fourth man, younger than the others, wore a corduroy jacket and pressed jeans. He leaned his chair onto its back legs, rocking away from the jumble of dishes, silverware and cups.

"This what you call high living, Sampson? Eating store-bought bread with your dinner?"

He grinned as he spoke, looking to the trooper on his right and the deputy on his left for some indication that his joke was shared. None came.

The city cop across the table was bull-necked, the sleeves of his uniform stretched at the shoulders and biceps. He spoke slowly, almost under his breath.

"You don't know how bad it bothers me that things around here don't suit you."

The younger man looked away, shaking his head slowly, side to side. He whispered, as if appealing to some invisible ally, some unseen source of reason. "God, you've got some chip on your shoulder."

Then silence with the younger man still looking away and the city cop waiting, waiting. The old deputy looked at the city cop who only stared at the younger man.

"Hey Betty, bring coffee," the deputy hollered. He hunkered toward the younger man to speak to him alone.

"How long you been down here, Mark?"

The younger man still gazed at the far wall. "About ninety years," he said.

On the far wall was a picture of Christ praying at Gethsemane. The picture was dark and the room dark and the reflection in the glass of the movement at the back door was almost indistinguishable from the picture, almost as if something in the picture itself had begun to move.

The younger man felt a stream of cool air on his neck. On impulse he looked not around but into the eyes of the city cop who faced him. There was no information in those eyes, and the younger man snapped his head around, flexing his right foot to feel against his leg the press of the revolver hanging inside his boot.

A young woman entered the room. She was looking at the floor and choking back giggles. She pulled the door shut with both hands, tugging hard to squeeze it into the ill-fitting frame. With the back of her hand she fluffed her hair out from under a denim jacket. Her hair was past the shoulder and weary from bleach and curling agents. The younger man felt the cold from her clothes and saw a gloss from the night air on her face. She was nearest him as she adjusted herself, preening, standing with one foot a bit forward for emphasis on her legs. The jeans hid nothing about them. They were good legs, dancer's legs. The smells were familiar: perfume, cigarettes, breath mints, beer, marihuana. She looked into the jukebox, her hand on the machine, rings clicking slowly against the glass. She frowned, then walked, as if down a fashion show runway, to the city cop's side. She bumped against him with her hip.

"Make room."

Jack Sampson scooted his chair away from the table and turned it slightly toward the woman. She sat in his lap. If she had noticed there were three other people in the room, she gave no sign of it. No fleeting moment of embarrassment, no nervous, self-conscious glances at the others.

"How you been, Jack? I never do see you around anymore."

The younger man emphasized a look at his watch. "I got to get on back," he said.

"What's wrong with your friend, Jack?" she said. "He still afraid of girls?"

THE YOUNGER man was gone with little sound—the feet of the chair sliding against the floor, a clank of a fork—and no words. He had driven four miles east before he wheeled his Chevrolet around and back-tracked to the restaurant. The parking lot was empty now, but yellow light still shone in the irregular windows, each pair a product of another add-on to the asymmetrical building.

Gene, skinny and grey, was at the counter, sorting the day's cash. His cigarette rested in a glass ashtray, its smoke rising in a straight column beside the cash register.

"Sorry, Gene. I forgot my check." The younger man had his wallet in hand.

"It's all right," Gene croaked. He did not look up. "Dep'ty Maddux got your'n."

The young man tapped his wallet against the counter, began to turn away, paused, and again focused on the old man who still did not look up.

"Thanks, Gene. Sorry."

"Don't thank me," the old man said as the younger man slipped through the door, back into the darkness.

"Who are you?"

The whispered demand came from darker darkness under the shadow of the restaurant. The younger man turned from the car. He could see only a faint silhouette, a shadow within a shadow—a woman sitting on the gravel lot, her back against the wall of the restaurant. The hair tucked under the jacket was a giveaway.

"I don't guess that's any of your business."

"It's my business." She snickered. "You just don't know what my business is."

"I don't care what your business is, honey."

The younger man turned away from her and focused on a ring of keys he held up toward the solitary streetlight.

"You don't, huh? Well let me tell you something. I *know* who you are. You're Mark Varner. You're a policeman down here from Charleston investigatin' who killed John Helton. You been down here since early summer and you still ain't got shit."

Varner had the door to the Chevy open. The interior light gave him a dim picture of her face.

"Now, see there, you really do know something."

Varner gripped the steering wheel and began to settle into the seat.

"I know a lot of things."

She stood and before he had started the engine she was resting her arms on the door of the Chevy. Her face against the window glass now, her eyes bearing the marks of the far country—overwide, glazed, red-streaked. Crazy eyes.

"I need a ride."

"Sorry, honey."

Varner slid the Chevy out from under her arms gently, fearing her collapse. She did not fall but rather seemed to deflate into a sloppy version of the lotus position—a slumping, boneless mass, unfazed by the widening shaft of light as the cruiser backed onto the asphalt road.

The cruiser turned toward Bandy. In Varner's rear view mirror the girl's back took the look of an old round-top tombstone marking a lone grave. A grey marker against an unbroken plane of black cinder. Varner considered calling Sampson. Sampson obviously knew this girl. He would know if anything needed to be done for her. But he decided not. Sampson would put any humanitarian concern behind a chance to berate him, to sabotage him. This was a tar baby sitting in the road. Sampson would see that and have himself a good time with it, particularly if it could be had at Varner's expense.

Five minutes later she was lying on her side, still immune to the headlights as Varner pulled the Chevy back onto the lot. The car crept toward the body, cinders crunching beneath the slow-rolling tires. The car stopped, its engine noise the heavy breath of a predator, its headlights eyes glowing over the prostrate body.

Varner pressed two fingers against the side of her throat. There was a pulse. Her make-up was smeared and exaggerated—the face of a sad clown.

"Come on, honey. Let's get you home. How much of that evil weed did you smoke?"

As Varner lifted her from the cinders, the girl's neck was slack, her head dangling and bouncing with each of his steps. His arms under her shoulders, under her thighs. Firm thighs. She made an attempt at words—a sloppy babble. A low fog had already begun to form, white wisps curling like pipe smoke in the high-beam lights, the dampness amplifying the omnipresent smell of sulphur. On the mountainside across the valley a conveyor belt stretched half-a-mile from top to bottom, lit every hundred yards with mercury lamps. From this distance it gave the appearance of a ski run.

She slumped as he placed her in the passenger seat, the seatbelt across her chest holding her from complete collapse. Varner turned the air conditioner on full and tilted a vent into her face. He pulled back onto the road.

"Where do you live, honey? You go home with me you're going to sleep it off in jail."

"No," she mumbled, her body still motionless, a limp marionette suspended by the single strand of the shoulder belt.

"Now, that's a start. Let's try a multiple choice. We're driving south into town. Is this the way to your house, or should we be going the other way?"

"Other way."

Varner slowed, found a wide spot and turned the cruiser around, headlight beams sweeping through pines, across a long, weedy lawn sloping down from the road, across a tiny white frame house, another small house, a rusty pickup truck, a shed.

"Now it gets harder. You're going to have to tell me where to stop or where to turn off, Cinderella, because at ten o'clock this cruiser has to be back at the barracks or it turns into a pumpkin. We've got half an hour to get you home. What that means is that you're going to have to get it together. Hold your head up so you can see out the windshield."

"Ain't you funny."

"I guess I am. I do seem to find my way into the funniest situations."

"You got a radio?"

"Yeah. But it won't do us any good. I can't transmit anywhere while we're stuck between these mountains. Nobody's listening here after five a clock, anyway. We could find a phone, there's bound to be a phone within ten miles or so…"

"I mean a music radio."

"This is not a party, Cinderella. Where do you live?"

"Music will wake me up. Rock n' roll."

"Your wish is my command."

"Not that station, dammit. Go on up. Go on up the dial. There. Now turn it up. Turn it up, dammit."

The song was one about a bird you cannot change. It was in the latter movement where all was guitar licks, whiny treble at machine-gun speed, a repetitive pumping that seemed to enter and possess the till-then limp body in the passenger seat.

"Crank it," she yelled.

She did not open her eyes, but her face focused and she jerked her forehead forward with the beat. Varner slowed the car and let the song finish in its blaze of glory. He reached for the volume control. She grabbed his hand. He yelled over the pattering disk jockey.

"This party is over. Tell me where you live, or I'm takin' you to jail."

"I could give you a real good party. You'd like me. I know you. I know what you'd like."

Varner stopped the cruiser.

"We're going to jail."

He began to turn the cruiser around without hesitation or much of a look around. They had not passed another car since leaving Gene's.

"Stop it." She was upright now. Bolt upright, one hand clutching the dash. "Just stop it, will you? I'll show you where I live. It's just over the next ridge. Across that bridge."

Varner shifted to reverse and undid his half-turn.

"I don't see why you have to be so serious all the time."

"What do you mean *all the time*? You don't know me. You haven't…"

"You'd be surprised at what I do know. Here. Stop here. You can let me out here."

She had the door open before the cruiser was completely stopped. She unbelted herself quickly and hopped onto the pavement. There was no sluggishness or lack of balance now. There was a break in the woods on the left side of the road, the break maybe large enough for a dirt road, but one he had never noticed before during his seven months in the county. She flashed like a vision through the headlights, bolting for the break like a schoolgirl in a game. Varner rolled down the window and yelled into the thickening fog.

"Who are you?"

The answer faded, word for word, into the woods.

"You'll find out."

3

The lights were on inside the barracks, almost all of them. He had purposely left them on when he left before dusk and would leave them on the rest of the night in the hope, now seemingly naive, that there was some portion of the troublemaking public in this county who did not know how alone he was.

He hung his jacket, emptied his pockets onto a dresser, and dropped onto a low bunk. A phone was on a table at the head of the bunk. He reached back overhead for it, set it on his belly and punched a series of digits.

"Hello," she said.

"Hey. How you doin'?"

"I'm fine." She hesitated. "I could be better."

He made a one beat sound, an exhale, a sarcastic laugh, somewhere between a snort and a snicker. "I could be better, too. How's Jamie?"

"He's fine. Jane brought Bobby over this evening. They played soldier. They were wild."

"Good. That's good."

"How's the case?"

"Not great."

There were several consecutive, breath-long pauses: She, sitting, staring at a cluttered kitchen counter, waiting for more of an answer, not knowing exactly how to respond, how not to sound impatient. Then he, pressing his lips together, toying with the phone cord, awaiting a response, not wanting to sound despairing. Then she again, considering the meaning of his now obvious pause, how it should affect her response. Then he, reading her silence as anger, frustration, hurt, thinking a longer pause would seem like a demand for a response. Should he demand?

"So...what's...going to happen?" she said.

"I don't know. I really don't know how long they will want to work this one. The strike and all...I don't know. This damn strike...."

"Any more violence?"

"The same stuff. Rock throwing on the picket line. No more shooting."

And on it went, a conversation on autopilot. It was a feeling he remembered. And it was a disturbing remembrance—an absence of sensation, as if the words had gone directly from idea to memory, as if the sounds were only there and only registered to let them know there were no surprises and that all had gone as programmed. A dance without touching.

Almost. The part of the conversation that *did* stick with Varner, that stayed with him like a bad meal as he laid in the bunk staring up into the darkness of the one unlit room, was the part about Jane's husband. He was an insurance agent. No hazardous duty. Work your own hours. Get paid for what you sell. *Develop a clientele*. Make money. He got a big bonus last month. They are adding on. *His firm is recruiting new agents*, she said. *They'll send you to school.*

There was no defense to this not-so-subtle prodding. *No, I like police work. I like being stuck in the middle of nowhere with a war going on and no help and a dead case and everybody and their brother lying to me and trying to find out what I've got and all for short pay.* It made the insurance business look like inheriting an earldom.

His answers to her were not what he wanted them to be. They were a little dishonest—*That's great. Oh really, that much? Their house would look great with a deck.* There was no non-juvenile justification for any other kind of response though—nothing in reality to support any protest he might try to make.

4

When he heard the phone he wondered how many times it had rung before it woke him. It was the public line ringing and it rang only at the desk in the office, not in the bunkroom. The clock said 5:50. An hour before daylight. The hoot owl shift would be leaving about now, maybe there were problems on a picket line somewhere. He threw back the covers and ran down the hallway for the office.

"State Police, Whitesville Detachment."

"Hi."

"Who is this?"

"This is Cinderella."

Varner sat down on the metal desktop and with his free hand pinched his brow.

"I hope you've got a good reason for getting me out of bed."

"You are such a smartass. That what happens to you when you get to be a cop? You get to be rude to people? You're going to be nice to me. I do have a reason, a good reason." "I'll be nice to you. What's your reason?"

"I know who killed John Helton."

"That's a good reason. Who killed him?"

Varner pulled open the middle desk drawer and from layers of clutter fished out a ball-point pen and a legal pad.

23

"My husband."

Varner shifted, pressing the phone against his ear with his shoulder, poised to write.

"What's your husband's name, ma'am?"

"Don't you ma'am me."

"Okay. What's your name?"

"Tonya."

"Tonya what?"

"Don't you know how to be nice," she screamed. "Don't you know how to talk to a woman? You were pretty rude to me last night, too."

"Okay, Tonya. I like that name. I'd like to know your last name, too."

"It's all you can bring yourself to do to be polite, ain't it? My last name's Dawson."

"Is your husband named Sam, Tonya?"

"That's him."

"He's a big guy."

"You scared of him?"

"There'd be times and places I would be. How do I know you're not bullshitting me, Tonya? Did you see it happen?"

"Smartass. I guess women bullshit you all the time about their husband's murdering somebody."

"You wouldn't believe the bullshit I get, Tonya. You got any evidence?"

"I've got the gun."

"That'll do it. Do you want to give me the gun?"

"Is anybody else there?"

"Just me."

"I'll be right there."

"Wait, Tonya—can I get your phone number there?"

"Don't you ever call me here. I've got to go."

As he heard her hang up, he pushed the other line button on the phone. He punched 8 for long distance, then a ten-digit number.

"This is Corporal Varner, Mrs. Winter. Can the Captain come to the phone? I'm sorry to have bothered you ma'am."

Varner stood and while holding the phone switched off the office lights. So hidden, he stared through the front window of the barracks. It was a large picture window and obviously makeshift as its squared top corners clashed against the arched ceiling line of the quonset-hut barracks. Outside, a naked, sulfur-colored bulb dangled from an iron fixture just over the window. It was still burning, its light a poisonous phosphorescent sphere submerged in a dark and stagnant sea of fog.

"Hello."

"Captain...."

"Mark?"

"Yes sir."

"What's up?"

"I might have the thing solved. I just got a tip. Some woman named Tonya Dawson just called. Says her husband killed Helton."

"That's Sam."

"Yeah."

"That don't make sense."

"Why's that?"

"Sam Dawson's a union man. He was president of one of the Locals down there a few years back. I expect he's killed people, but one union man don't murder another in the middle of a strike like this. Even if Dawson'd a'wanted Helton dead he'd a'waited till after the strike was over."

"She says she has the gun."

"That'll make it easy. She gonna give you the gun?"

"Says she is. Says she's bringing it here now."

"Anybody there with you?"

"No."

"Remember the last woman who wanted to solve a crime for you?"

"Yeah."

"Then you watch the hell out. I say it ain't him."

"Captain, why is *everybody* down here crazy?"

"They ain't crazy. They's just mad. You'd a'had to live there to know."

Varner saw the headlights rush valkyrie-like through the fog and nearly into the picture window. Two short blasts from the car horn, then a long, uninterrupted whine.

"I got to go, Captain. She's here."

Varner dropped the phone, pulled an unholstered revolver from a low drawer and went through the front door. The car was a new; sleek, red, and low slung. Tonya Dawson was driving, another woman, a dark brunette, riding shotgun. From the front stoop of the quonset he yelled, *"Lay off that horn."*

When the horn stopped, there was no relief. Now the shrieks of some pop diva blared from inside the car. The corporal waved his arms like he was signaling an airliner to a halt.

"Turn that thing down," he yelled again.

Tonya Dawson bent over in her driver's seat. The heads of the two women came together. They were giggling, talking, moving with the blaring music. Tonya Dawson turned away from her friend and pointed a blue-steel revolver out of the driver's window and at Varner.

"I'm not turning it off. I love this song." She was laughing.

Varner leaped headlong back through the open barracks door, belly-sliding across the worn floorboards. He yelled at the top of his lungs. "You drop that gun! You drop that damn gun right now or you're a dead woman—both of you!"

The music stopped.

"Nobody's gonna hurt you, honey. I just brought this for you to check out."

The gun sailed through the door, spinning like a thrown knife. Varner winced as it skipped across the floor, stopping inches in front of his nose.

"There's your murder weapon, honey," she yelled.

The woman slammed the car into reverse and gunned the engine, spinning the tires and sending slag and cinders pinging against the picture window and through the doorway. Varner slid into the doorway, and trained his revolver on the car.

"Stop it. Hold it right there. You're under arrest—I'll shoot."

The red car jerked to a halt. Tonya leaned through the open window, tilting her head, prissy and mocking.

"You ain't shooting nobody, Corporal. If you want me, come and arrest me. I might like that sometime. Right now, though, I'm heading home before Sam gets home from work. *He will* kill me if he finds out I'm here. He'd kill you, too—in a heartbeat." Her voice was getting steadily louder as she continued. Now she paused, closed her eyes, and yelled at the top of her lungs. "I can make your murder case for you. You get that gun tested or whatever and get it back to me tonight."

"Okay, okay." Varner lowered the revolver and walked toward the red car. "Where and when, Tonya? Just tell me where and when."

"Sam's got picket duty tonight. He'll be looking for it at around seven. Bring it to me at Joe's Creek tonight before six-thirty. You come alone. Sam owns every other cop in this county—I hope you at least know that."

Tonya Dawson pulled the car onto the blacktop road. She and her passenger were laughing again. The girls' heads came together for a moment as the car paused, now pointing to the onlooking officer's right. Tonya Dawson leaned across the other girl, rolled down the passenger side window and yelled again.

"You're awful cute in your shorts, Corporal."

5

Varner gripped the steering wheel and stared at the rear end of the coal truck ten feet ahead. The side of the overwide truck bed brushed against an overhanging oak branch and pulled it along, bending it like a bow. The leafy branch slid in steps along the waffled side of the bed. Then, as the truck passed, the branch whipped back, quivering and pointing like an angry hand. The truck stopped to downshift as the grade steepened, then jerked ahead, shuddering and spilling a thin stream of glossy black pebbles onto the tattered asphalt and the hood of the cruiser.

He looked into the rear-view mirror. Four cars, then another overloaded truck, all moving at tortoise speed. He banged the heel of his hand against the steering wheel and imagined the steep road crumbling under the weight of the vehicles that seemed to pull against it, the ragged ribbon of asphalt disintegrating like a rotten rope and falling with the slow climbers down the side of the mountain.

Over the mountain the road widened and the woods were cut away farther from the pavement. There was an open stretch long enough to pass in and a few miles later traffic had adjusted. Ahead, at the Short Creek bridge, Varner could make out figures—several large, bearded men with camouflage hats and jackets.

Varner unhooked a microphone from the cruiser's console and pressed the switch.

"Four twenty-one to Charleston."

"This is Charleston," a woman replied.

"I'm approaching marker forty-five on route twenty-one. I've got activity at the Short Creek bridge."

"Is that strike activity, four-twenty-one?"

"It looks like it from here. I'm not on it yet. You got any other report?"

"No. Not there or anywhere else today. Anything look funny?"

"Yeah. It looks funny. Seven or eight men standing around the bridge doing nothing. I'm not going to stop unless I have to. Where's my closest back-up unit, Charleston?"

There was no immediate answer. Varner slowed the cruiser.

"Four-twenty-one, I've got three-eighteen five miles your side of Beckley."

"Then I'm not stopping even if I have to. I'm there now. I'm right up on 'em. Nothing. They aren't even looking at me. Weird."

"They picketers?"

"No signs. I don't see any signs. There's no mine entrance around here that I know of."

"You through it four-twenty-one? I've got some other callers here."

"Yeah. I'm through. I'm fine. Hey, before you get off...tell the ballistics lab I'm on my way in. I've got to get a gun tested today. Could you have somebody stand by? I've got to have it done today. It's an emergency."

"Everything's an emergency these days, four-twenty-one. I'll do what I can. When you going to be here?"

"I don't know. I meant to be there already. I'm pushing it as it is. I'll be there in another hour unless this traffic gets pinched up again."

THERE WERE two men in the office when Varner passed the booking window. Both were in uniform. The older man, who was overweight, was leaning back in an office chair with his feet propped on a desk. The younger man, who was standing, lifted his chin toward Varner.

"Hey, Mark. Thought you were still down on the strike murder."

"I got to get a ballistics done." He lifted a revolver inside a plastic bag. "Winter around?"

"He's upstairs. That the murder weapon?"

"I've got somebody telling me it is. Is anybody down at ballistics?"

"Sandy was around earlier. I don't know if she's gone yet."

Varner walked quickly across the parking lot of the headquarters complex, across a lawn and around a pistol range to a long, low, flatroofed building. The door was standing open.

"Sandy?"

"I'm in the middle of something, Mark." Her voice came from behind an interior door. "Lay your emergency on the counter there. I'll get it next."

"Ah...Sandy, when's next? I've got to get this thing back tonight."

A young woman opened the interior door. She wore a white lab coat, goggles, and latex gloves. Her hair was pulled back in a net.

"Next is just next. That's all. Fill out the custody slip and leave it on the counter. If you've got a complaint, there are forms for that, too. I'll call you when I'm done. Where are you going to be?"

"Winter's office. Upstairs."

The woman disappeared behind the door. Varner stood in the middle of the empty waiting area. Surrounded by a mix of vinyl-covered chairs, he weighed the bagged gun in his left hand. He was motionless until the pungent chemical smell reached him. He winced, laid his package on the counter and left the building.

"THEM BALLISTICS won't match up," Winter said as he squirted tobacco juice into a white foam cup. "They ain't no way. I know Dawson and I knowed

Helton. Either one of 'em'd kill the other'n. Wouldn't surprise nobody. But not in the middle of no strike."

Varner took a swig from a can of Pepsi. "You're always right," Varner grinned, "but I hope you're wrong this time."

The room was a corner room on the second and top floor of the building. There were tall windows in both outside walls, through them the white sky was split by power lines, thick, black and close. Jail windows turned sideways. Varner rested against a window sill. Winter, in uniform, jug-eared, ham-handed, crew-cut, square-shouldered, square jaw bulging with chew, sat in his desk chair. Physical discipline still holding a short lead over age.

"I ain't wrong and this is bullshit. I don't like doin' no investigation with all the world lookin' over your shoulder. It don't work that way at all. Things has got to be looser. You got to be able to lay low for awhile, catch somebody lookin' the other way. But nobody don't understand that. Not anymore, they don't. This Department. I'll tell you, anymore bein' a trooper don't mean nothin'. It's just like havin' a job."

Winter laid his hands, palms down, on his desk. They were shaking. He looked back at Varner and spoke in a lower tone.

"What did Dawson's wife tell you?"

"She just said he did it. He did it and she had the gun. I haven't had much chance to talk to her."

"She say why he did it?"

"No. Why would she lie about it?"

"Oh, they could be lots a' reasons. She might even half believe it herself. But it's fun for her to do—mess around in an investigation. It's like bein' in a movie. What else you think she's got to do durin' the day?"

"It seems so crazy. What a risk. What if he'd find out she talked?"

"'That's part a' the fun of it. Part a' the movie."

Winter pushed back in his desk chair and again lifted the foam cup to his lower lip and expertly squirted a stream of tobacco juice into the cup. He righted the chair and spoke.

"You been in touch with the U. S. Attorney's Office about this?"

"No. It just happened. I've been on the run since I found out about it."

"You need to call 'em. They get snippy if you don't. They like to think they're in charge of things all along."

"What happens if I don't?"

"It'll be easier for 'em to tell you why they ain't gonna prosecute the case."

"Who do I talk to, up there?"

"Sally Thomas."

"Who is Sally Thomas?"

"She's been there three or four years now, I reckon. I've worked cases with her before. She's tough, and she ain't afraid to go to trial."

The phone on Winter's desk buzzed. He raised his eyebrows and cracked the barest smile.

"That's Sandy to tell us it ain't the gun."

"Winter. Yeah, he's right here lookin' at me. Yeah, well, I already knew that, but I'll tell him. Yeah, he'll be right down."

AS VARNER opened the lab door he saw the revolver and five mangled bullets laying on a white cloth on the counter. The young woman was standing behind the counter, writing on paper in a clipboard. She did not look up as she spoke.

"You want the short version, I guess."

"That's fine."

The woman pointed with her pen to the three bullets on her right.

"I'm told these three slugs were taken out of the body. These three over here are from your gun. They don't match. They're close, but this is not the murder weapon."

"How close?"

"Almost exactly the same. In fact, I think this is the same kind of gun that the killer used. But it wasn't this gun."

"How are you so sure?"

"This gun is a Walton-Martin. Made over in Ohio. It's a very cheap gun. Most manufacturers test fire their guns after they're made, but Walton-Martin saves a few quarters and doesn't do any test firing. I dropped some chemical on the receiver here to identify any gunshot residue." She held the gun and tapped her finger on a spot immediately behind the cylinder. "None showed.

"That might only mean that it has been thoroughly cleaned since the last time it was fired. But, without the test fires, you've got some very tiny ragged spots still in the barrel from the rifling tool. And there's another thing about Walton-Martin. They're sloppy about how they finish the end of the barrel. After they do the rifling, they don't do much to polish off the barrel end. The result of both of those things is that the first couple of bullets that come through the barrel do the cleaning and polishing." She set the gun back onto the table.

"I fired that gun twelve times. There are little flecks of barrel steel on the first five of these bullets. Then the bullets look normal—like you'd expect them to look otherwise. These test shots are the first bullets to ever come out of this gun, Mark. I'll bet my paycheck on that."

6

Varner knocked on the door before using his key, but there was no answer and he heard no stirring in the house. He stood on the front stoop and turned away from the door into the late afternoon sun. A bicycle was laying in the grass, a baseball cap beside it. He took his keys from his pocket and slid one into the lock then turned his head to his right, toward the breezeway and garage where his three year old son appeared. The boy was dripping wet and carrying the flowing end of a garden hose.

"Hey, Dad—you're home." The child looked back into the breezeway. "Hey, Mom; Dad's home."

He pulled the key from the lock and went through the breezeway where he met his wife coming toward him. She wore a straw hat and sunglasses. He put his arms around her waist and kissed her and she accepted the kiss. She took his hand and they walked into the back-yard where a single folding lawn chair stood. There was a glass of ice and an open magazine beneath the chair.

"I didn't know you were coming," she said. "Dinner is on, and it's not much."

"I didn't either, 'til just a little while ago. I can't stay. I've got to get back tonight."

She looked away from him and did not respond.

That said everything. They went on from there, the three of them. Through the motions. There were lots of words of encouragement and praise for the boy. The little bit of dinner was made to do. Dana was Dana. She knew who she was and she knew the deal. It was unjust to complain, especially now. He did have real work to do, and sending him away upset would start a chain of events that would later be hard to stop.

But Mark knew Dana, too. Knew how well she knew the deal and just how careful she was not to presume or expect anything more. But the look away, the split second of frustration and disappointment not quite hidden. He knew her well enough to know what that meant. There was so much there, so much brewing within her that she, the master of herself, the master of her own emotions, the world's best at not letting the word slip, so much there that in that tiny moment, that turn of the head, that lack of a pert response, she had betrayed it.

What she would have said if it had not been unfair, a violation of the deal, to say it, Mark well knew. You are missing the best of it, she would have said. I don't completely understand, maybe, whatever it is that draws you to this work, and I know that any other job would have its problems and inconveniences, but whatever else may be, you are missing the best of life. Here I am, she would have said, in my very prime, for you. Here is your son, your very image, here for you. Do you not understand, she would say, how much we need you? How very particular our need for you is? There are hundreds of policemen that could do that job in Boone County, but only one husband and father in this house. Do you not understand how urgent this is? That these days of ours when health is good and life is sweet are passing? Do you not see what the boy needs from you? Those things that no one else will ever give him?

She did not say these things, he knew, because of the deal, and because if he did not see these things himself, then what was the use? If these things of beauty were not beautiful to him, if they did not call him more strongly away from whatever else held his attentions, then what was the good in talking about it?

This is what he knew she thought as he left his home, waved goodbye, and headed south for Boone County and the barracks.

7

It was twenty after six and nearly dusk when he hit the logjam of coal trucks and cars about a mile north of Short Creek. Varner pulled the red light from under his seat and stuck it on the dash. He wheeled the cruiser into the empty northbound lane, light flashing, and began to inch down the mountain, passing the frozen parade of cars and giant trucks. As he passed a switchback turn, other oscillating red lights came into view. Varner, seeing his way clear to the head of the stopped traffic and to the cluster of cruisers and emergency vehicles, lifted his foot from the brake and coasted to the clearing where, only hours ago, the Short Creek bridge had stood. He recognized Beak Barnes, a uniformed man with whom he had served several years ago in the eastern panhandle. The silhouette was unmistakable: one-hundred sixty pounds spread over six feet four inches with twin peaks of a nose and Adam's apple.

"Hey, Barnes," Varner called, "what the hell happened here?"

"Do you guys in investigations turn your radios in with your uniforms? What does it look like happened, anyway?"

"Somebody blew up the bridge."

"That's why they pick you guys for investigations isn't it—your amazing powers of perception."

Varner got out of the car and walked to the creek bank. He looked down at the massive truck on its side twenty feet below. The load of coal, now spilled out upstream from the truck, made a black island in the middle of the rushing stream.

"Driver get out okay?" he yelled back to Barnes.

"They think so. He was scraped up pretty bad. Lost some blood. They're going to look at him for awhile."

Varner kicked a soap bar-sized fragment of asphalt over the jagged ledge left at the end of the pavement. It dropped without spinning, giving a dreamy, knuckle-ball illusion of suspension as it fell. The stream swallowed it with a hollow *poomf.*

"I'm going to have to leave this cruiser here, Barnes. Will there be security here tonight?"

"You're looking at it. Why are you leaving the cruiser? You going for a walk or something?"

"No. I've got to radio somebody on the other side to come pick me up. I've got an appointment I can't miss tonight."

Varner saw that Barnes was making no attempt to hide a scowl.

"It's strike-related," Varner said.

"Forget that. All the troops are in the woods, man. The guys that did this are up on that mountainside over there." Barnes pointed across the creek. "We've had sniper fire. We're dug in like an army, buddy. The National Guard is on alert. There is nobody around to carry you to your date, Corporal." Then Barnes gave his narrow face an exaggerated tilt and faked a British accent: "Shall I call a cab for you, officer?"

VARNER PULLED the cruiser off the road and onto a worn spot—a collection of question-mark-shaped ruts on the right made by trucks turning wide to go left into Joe's Creek hollow. He jammed the shift lever into park and dropped his head back against the headrest. He looked at his watch, then closed his eyes and pressed his fingers against his eyelids. He blew out a long breath. Beside him in the seat were three empty foam cups—dead soldiers, angling against the seat-back, each with its own set of commercial tattoos. The moonlight favored the pale whiteness of the cups, seeming to pick them out and render them luminous against the seat and clutter.

Varner straightened up in the seat and arched his neck over the top of the headrest. He ran his hands over his head then back to his closed eyes. He settled back into the seat and dropped his hands. He sighed, then sat motionless, eyes still shut, for minutes. Then his head jerked slightly and he opened his eyes and again looked at his watch. He shifted into drive.

Varner turned the Chevy left, off of the blacktop and onto, or rather into, the single set of deep ruts that was

Joe's Creek road. The Chevy's rear bumper scraped the asphalt as the back wheels dropped into the ruts. The road was dry now, but its complexion had been formed in mud and bore deep, encrusted tire prints, sharp ridges and pinnacles, the calcified results of mud slung, pressed, and pushed by hurrying mammoth vehicles.

The car was now fixed on its course and had no more freedom from this road than a train from its track. Varner kept the car at the speed of a stalking cat, now and then the high middle of the road scraping loudly against the underside of the Chevy.

White oaks and maples overhung the road, their leafy branches meeting and crossing overhead, completing dense archways, blocking the stars. The road wound up the mountainside. A mile in, still heading uphill, Varner pulled his foot from the gas and braked. He pushed in the headlight switch and the thin tunnel of light before him collapsed. Varner looked right, left and into the rear view mirror. As a lightning bolt maps a distant sky and dies, leaving not an unbroken sky but the absence of sky, the absence of distance, so here there was no relief, no distinction, no distance. He rolled down the window and reached for the ignition. A jingle of the dangling keys, the murmur of the idling engine. He rested his thumb on the ignition key, his fingers on the column, for minutes. He did not kill the engine. He pulled the light switch and checked the fuel gauge. Half tank. The car began to creep forward again.

On top of the mountain the road opened onto an abandoned strip mine. The road was unrutted here—covered with layer upon layer of slag and red-dog—and the land clear and level as a football field. As Varner wheeled the Chevy off of the road, the high-beams shot the perimeter of the clearing revealing a few small shacks, some mounds of shale, and distant steel machines. These were gigantic machines, big as buildings, their uplifted arms as frozen and unrepentant as Lot's wife. They cast strange, Jurassic shadows across the ruined soil.

The engine off, Varner could hear wind rustling in the trees. He pulled a revolver from a holster beneath his seat, stuffed it into the front of his jeans, pocketed his keys, and left the car. He walked to the side of the headlight beams, continuing in his original direction down the road. He had not gone twenty paces when he heard the back window of the Chevy shatter. He pulled the gun and pivoted toward the noise and into the glare of the headlights. He dropped to prone and rolled away from the light beams. Listening and struggling to see, he lay on his belly, arms extended before him, both hands gripping the revolver.

He saw nothing, and when he heard the scream it was too late. It came from nowhere—certainly not from the direction of the car, not from the direction that any rock that had smashed the rear window had come. And then it was on him, teeth slashing into the edge of his ear, pain like a burn from a hot iron, arm around his neck, elbow at his throat, squeezing closed. He was choking.

Varner dropped the revolver and reached both hands behind his head, seizing the neck of his attacker, pressing his thumbs into the throat, death gripping. Five seconds. Ten seconds. The arm around his neck went slack.

"Let me go," she choked.

"Is anybody else here?"

"Lemmego," she gasped.

"Put your hands on my head. Easy."

Varner released her neck and grabbed her offered wrists.

"Is there anybody else here?"

"No, god damn it. It's just me, you son of a bitch. You god damned liar."

"I'm going to let go of your left hand. You roll off me, onto your back."

She slithered off of him inch by inch, wiggling, pressing her breasts into his back. With her free hand, she stroked his side.

"Ooh-ooh," she moaned. "Am I gonna get it, now? You gonna give it to me?"

"You're gonna get jail is what you're gonna get."

Tonya Dawson, sitting now, and still attached to Varner at the wrist, again went rigid. "Oh, I'm gonna get jail, huh? You're the one that deserves jail. I give you your case, give up my husband, and you stand me up. You don't get here till midnight. What do you think

I did when Sam got home six hours ago and his damned gun wasn't there? You think he liked that okay? You think he was pretty cool about that, Mr. Trooper? You'd better look at me. You better have a damn look at me before *you* take *me* anywhere."

They were by now sitting ten yards outside the light beams and Varner could see only outlines. She had gotten her hair cut. It was shoulder length now and curled under, and she was wearing a dress.

"Get in the car," he ordered.

He stood and pulled her up by the wrist. Blood dripped from the cuts on his ear onto her dress. His arm quivered as he accepted her weight.

"That gun isn't the one," he said.

In the interior light he saw that the dress was red. A loose fitting, thin dress. The hem lay slack and billowy half way above her knees as she sat again in the passenger seat. She played with the hem as she sat, both hands lifting and sliding it up and down her slender legs. She was leaning back into the seat, her head against the headrest, looking away from Varner and into the window, her legs spread apart.

"How do you like my haircut?" She asked.

"Why did you jump me?"

"I was mad at you, dammit. Look at this."

She turned her head to face him and pushed her face in front of his. She pointed to her right eye. It was bloodshot, the flesh around it black and blue. Her index finger shook as she pointed.

Varner closed his eyes.

"I'm sorry. I am very sorry. I did everything I possibly could to get here on time. The Short Creek bridge is out. The Union blew it up. I've been on every bad road in ten counties in the last three hours."

"You want to see what else he did to me?" She began to unbutton the shirtdress. The top button was ripped.

"Don't you take that thing off."

She continued unbuttoning and did not look at Varner.

"What are you going to do to stop me? *You* gonna hit me, too?"

"No. I'm going to tell Sam on you. I've got his gun. I'm going to tell him where I got his gun."

She looked at him now, her hands frozen on the buttons. Her bra was visible. So was a fist-sized bruise just below her neck.

"He'll kill you."

"I can get reassigned. I can get out of here."

She began rebuttoning. "How do you like my haircut?"

"Why do you think Sam killed Helton?"

"I don't think he killed him. I know he did."

"How do you know? Were you with him when he did it?"

She rolled her eyes and shook her head. "I've got rights. You've gotta give me my rights."

Varner looked away, nodding his head. He spoke louder.

"Okay, Tonya. Here're your rights. You don't have to talk to me. You can get out of this car right now and go back into whatever tree you were in before you pounced on me. How's that, huh? How's that for rights?"

"That ain't all of 'em. I got a right to a lawyer."

Varner laughed. "There aren't any lawyers around here right now, Tonya. I'd bet on that."

"I still got a right to one."

Varner looked toward her now. He spoke softly, matter-of-factly. "That's right. And when you get out of this car, I'm going to go back to town and get a murder warrant for you and your husband both and I'm going to come and serve it on you. Then you can get a lawyer. Go on, get out."

She sat motionless—speechless, staring straightaway at the black windshield. She swallowed hard and swallowed hard again. She began to cry. Not sobbing, but flowing tears. She strained to control her voice.

"You've got to give me something."

"I can't give you anything."

"I'm going to give you something. You've got to give me something to get it. That's how it works. I know that. Everybody knows that."

"I can't give you anything."

"Yes, you can. It's how it works. You're just mad. You don't have to do this. You can give me something."

"Were you in on the murder?"

Her head dropped and she covered her face with her hands. She could not squelch what came out as a tiny cry, like that of a hurt child. She gasped for breath. Her head shook with her sobs. Varner rested his hand atop the steering wheel. His jaw was set, his ear still bloody.

"You in on it, Tonya?"

"No," she whimpered.

"Okay. Okay, Tonya. Listen to me. I can't promise you anything. You've got to remember that. I can promise you nothing. The promises are for the lawyers. I can tell you some things, though. Things that you'll want to know. You listening? Can you hear me, Tonya? You understand?"

"Yes." She nodded.

"Okay, then. Listen real close. You've just made a decision. There is no going back now. You've picked your team and the best thing you can do for yourself now is give it everything you've got. Don't hold anything back. You hold something back on me and you've shot yourself in the foot. You're fair game again. You come all the way for me, help me get Sam locked up, and I'll do everything I can for you."

"What can you do?"

"The prosecutor likes me. The prosecutor wants this case as bad as I do. She listens to me. I can make a case for you. What are you worried about? You got some exposure on something? You into something other than this murder?"

"Yes."

"Drugs?"

"Yes."

"Dealing?"

"Yes."

"With Sam?"

"Yes."

"Marijuana?"

"Yes."

"Local stuff? Grown around here?"

"Yes."

"How much?"

"About two hundred pounds. Last summer. Everybody around here does it. It's no big deal around here."

"You sell it around here or ship it out of state?"

"Here. All around here."

"Anything else?"

"No."

"Cocaine?"

"No. I wish."

She looked up at him, smiled quickly and began to fondle her dress hem again. "No, I don't wish that now."

"You're telling me two hundred pounds of marijuana? That's it? Nothing else?"

"Yeah."

"I think we can handle that, Tonya. You come across. You convince me you're doing everything you can, and I think things will work out fine for you on that. Tell me what you know."

"How do you like my hair?"

"We're not here to talk about your hair, Tonya. This isn't a game."

"You may be smart, trooper, but you can't snow the snow-woman. This is a damn game. That's exactly what it is. You want this information or not? How do you like my hair?"

Varner looked at the car ceiling. The dome light had drawn a grey moth. It fluttered, then lit on the dark fabric.

"Fine, Tonya. The hair is fine. Lovely. Now, tell me what you know."

"Oh, you snotty son of a bitch. She squinted and she sprayed spittle as she spoke. You like my hair. You like me. You were fighting yourself over whether you wanted this dress off of me or not. You like me. You like the way I look and you like this haircut. You're real proud that I'm after you, too. You know what you'll do when you get in the bed tonight, by yourself? You'll think about me. Don't think I don't know that."

Varner was turned toward her now, his elbow resting atop the steering wheel. He did not respond.

"Okay," she said, "but let's be all business, now. I know Sam killed Johnny because I know **why** he killed him."

"Okay. Why'd he kill him?"

"It was about a drug deal. You got a cigarette?"

"No."

"I knew it. Anyhow, Johnny owed Sam for a hundred pounds of pot. Johnny wouldn't pay. Sam kept goin' down to Johnny's trailer, threatenin' him. Threatenin' to kill Johnny. The guy from Ohio was on Sam's ass bad."

"What guy from Ohio?"

"The guy whose dope it was."

"You told me there was nothing interstate."

"We sold it all right here. We sold half of everything we got to Johnny. This guy from Ohio was a big guy. Even Sam was scared of him."

"How do you mean, big? Physically?"

"Physically and other ways, too. Sam said he was connected."

"So Sam's good buddy owes him for some dope and Sam kills him. Why'd he do that? That doesn't get him paid."

"It got the man from Ohio off of Sam's back. You have no idea how those people can be."

"Yes, I do. They can have you killed."

"That's not funny," she said. "I knew Johnny."

"Anything ever between you and Johnny?"

"Yeah."

"Before or after you married Sam?"

"Both."

"Sam know about that? That part of the motive here?"

"No. Sam never found out about the stuff after we were married. I do lots of things Sam don't know about."

"What about Jack Sampson? Anything between you and Officer Sampson?"

"What's that to you? He ain't got nothin' to do with this."

"You got something going with Sampson? You were awfully friendly with him last night."

"None of your business. Why? You jealous?"

"No. I'm not jealous. Just curious."

"You got something against Sampson? He kick your ass or somethin'?"

Varner ran a finger around the Chevrolet logo at the center of the steering wheel. "What are we going to do about Sam?"

"You tell me. You're the cop."

"He still dealing?"

"Yeah."

"Still getting it from the Ohio guy?"

"Yeah. He's letting Sam sell for him 'til he makes up for the money Johnny didn't pay."

"What's the Ohio guy's name?"

"Blackie Unrue."

"Is Blackie black?"

"No."

"Where's he out of? What city?"

"He ain't out of a city. He's out of Meigs County. They grow it there. That whole county is one big pot patch."

"You told me earlier that it was grown here."

"I said we sold it here."

"You said it was all locally grown."

"Meigs County is local. It's just across the river."

"I asked you if there was any out-of-state connection."

She exhaled audibly through her nose and looked into the car's ceiling.

"You havin' fun doin' this? You get a prize for winnin' a debate or somethin'?"

"How does Sam talk to Unrue?"

"Sometimes he comes here. Sometimes we go there."

"We?"

"Yeah. I usually go with him. Not so much now that the baby's here."

"Baby?"

"I've got a little boy. Seven months old. You wouldn't think that lookin' at me, would you?" She flexed and extended her arms, then moved them as if to music. "I do aerobics."

"How old are you, Tonya?"

"Twenty."

"He ever talk with Unrue over the phone?"

"Pay phones."

"You know Unrue's number?"

"Nope."

"You know where he lives?"

"I could get you there. It's way out in the country."

"Unrue a grower?"

"I'm not sure. People around him do. There's lots of them there. They're all friends. It's like a club."

"Do you know when Sam's going to see Unrue again?"

"No. Not for sure. It won't be long, though. Within a week."

"Can you go with him?"

"Probably. More than likely. All depends on whether I can get a sitter. And Sam is pissed at me right now. It's really hard to tell what he'll do. Hell, he might kill me."

"He's pissed at you because of the gun?"

"Yeah."

"What did you tell him?"

"I told him I gave it to my sister's husband. He's picketing, too. They'll cover for me. They cover for me all the time. They know how Sam is. What he does to me."

"They'll cover for you on this gun? What are you going to tell them?"

"I'll tell 'em I hid the thing 'cause I was afraid he'd use it on me. That ain't even a lie. What makes you so sure that ain't the gun?"

"I had it tested. That gun's never been shot before."

She slammed her back against the seat.

"You idiot. I *know* it's been shot before. It's been shot at me. I could show you the holes in the trailer."

Varner did not immediately respond. Looking down, he rubbed a palm across his forehead and held the other hand up and open as if preparing to raise it in inquiry.

"I believe you." He finally said. "At least I believe something about this story of yours. I don't think you'd be here otherwise."

"I might be here otherwise," she said. "But I am telling the truth."

"Problem is, nobody else will ever believe you. Not you alone, anyway. Are there any other witnesses to the drug stuff?"

"Nobody that would talk."

"Well, we got a problem, then."

"So, that's it? That's the end of the so-called investigation? You get a bad lab report and you just quit?"

"No. I know something else we can try."

"Okay."

"There are some problems with it. Some dangers."

"I've already got problems, and I'm already in danger."

"Open the glove box. There, get that black thing out." Varner pointed. "Let me show you. This is a body recorder. You wear this thing when you go with Sam to meet Unrue. Here's the on-off. This tape in here is blank. It'll last 90 minutes. Just leave it on. After you turn it on, leave it on. Don't turn it off. It'll go off by itself. If you turn it off, that may give you problems with your testimony."

"Put it on me. Show me how to put it on me." She smiled.

"Let me tell you something, Tonya. You are in this now. There's no screwing around. There'll be no screwing around. You've got to listen to me and do what I tell you. We've got to be very careful here. I lose this case and

I go to the next case. You lose this case, Sam doesn't go to jail and you get to live with him. You like that idea?"

"How do I put it on ?"

"Just put it in your purse. You carry a purse?"

"I can."

"When you make a tape, don't even take the tape out of the machine. Just bring me the machine and the tape back, just like they are now. Don't mess around with it."

"Okay. Okay. You finished?"

"Just about. The other thing is there will be no more wrestling matches. No more surprises out of you. You make the tape, call me, and we'll go from there. You understand that?"

"Yeah. I got to get goin'."

"You need a ride out of here?"

"No."

"How're you going to get home?"

"None of your business."

"Don't screw up, Tonya. I'm trusting you. You're in this more than I am."

9

How his first wife knew of the affair Varner never found out. She stood in the kitchen that summer afternoon, looking down at a newspaper on the counter. Dinner was not on, and she did not speak or look up when he entered the room. He stood still by the refrigerator.

"I know about it," she said. "I know about you and her. Don't lie to me anymore."

The first question *How did she find out* disappeared as quickly as it had rushed to consciousness. She knew, that was that. He could not control his thoughts or the merciless velocity of their attack. He did not know if he spoke or wept or became angry or how he appeared to her. This loss of control of his most essential functions was like vomiting. The thing came in waves, over his back and over his head and gripping and shaking him physically to exhaustion then releasing him and coming again.

All the rationalizations that had held him up in this wrong thing, that had been his way deeper into transgression, passed before him and broke soundlessly in that moment like so many wet reeds. There was no excuse and no plea.

After the divorce, his father said this, "There will be consequences because of this thing, but don't punish

yourself. It's God's business and He will see to it. Don't
you make things any harder than they really are for
yourself. It's not your place to do that, it doesn't get you
any extra points anywhere and you will lose your way.
You will not know, after a while, what is God's punish-
ment and what you have put upon yourself because you
wanted to—because you wanted to hate yourself. That's
wrong and it's a sin. If you are given tomorrow, you are
given it to live it. You have got to be honest and live life.
You've got some of that left, and it won't all be bad. You
might be surprised, if you just let yourself live."

And he decided to do just that. He would not calcu-
late to constrict the life he might have left to live, after
all. Like a man struck deaf and blind, he determined to
walk about and bump into things and to relearn the
landscape rather than sit still in the darkness that he
might have deserved, going from silence to coma to
death, as he might have deserved. And with each small
venture and with every collision the more he remembered how the world was and why men moved on the
earth and the bumps became softer and he went farther
and farther away from the dark room. There were
times when sight and sound seemed to return to him for
passing moments and then he was sane and to himself.
In these times he heard his own voice when he spoke
and he understood his own words and, once again, he
knew his own mind.

A place very far from this dark room was the Starlighter. It was a log roadhouse, just off Route 60, ten miles south of Beckley. The Walker family had run the place since World War II. Its dance floors were spacious and worn smooth everywhere and there was a stage for the band and lamplit booths along the walls and none of the manufactured atmosphere or the hard edges or kitsch or color-schemes of the post-strip-mall bars. There were screens inside the windows and in the summer they rolled the windows out and opened up the hall to the sweet night air.

The Starlighter was a favorite of the uniformed troops in all of Companies B and C—the Turnpike Company and the Beckley Field Office. That made thirty-some troops in all and there were always enough singles and divorcees and marrieds without childrens among them to fill two or three booths there late in the week. Six months to the day after the divorce decree was entered, he saw Dana at the Starlighter.

He first saw her on the dance floor. She was jitter-bugging with a slender man with glasses and a beard. She was laughing. She looked at Varner. She danced again, the next dance. This time with another man.

Steve Smithers, a uniform trooper from the Beckley Detachment came across the dance floor, pinching the mouth of a long-necked beer bottle with his thumb and forefinger. He was wearing jeans and a loud, western shirt. "She's looking at you," he said.

"I don't know. She's looking at a lot of things."

Smithers was grinning, almost laughing, at Varner. "Wrong. I learned a lot in polygraph school, Mark. I can tell."

"What can you tell?" Varner asked.

"Wait a second here. Wait till she stops dancing." Smithers nodded toward her. "You watch where she points her feet when she stands or sits down. She'll point them right at you, even if she's sitting the other way."

"What's that mean?"

"It means sincerity in a polygraph setting. It means the person is in contact with you. Here it means she wants to talk to you. Its an invitation to those who aren't too stupid to take it. She's not going to stare at you. It's impolite. So she does it in a way that's not so obvious. But it *is* obvious. You watch."

When the music stopped Dana moved to the far side of the house and to the bar and sat in a barstool. She faced the dance floor for a moment, then swiveled the stool around with her waist as if to order a drink. She kept her feet on the ring at the bottom of the stool, pointed at Varner.

Smithers looked at Varner and grinned again and raised his eyebrows. "I ought to get paid for this," he said.

Varner went to her and she smiled as she saw him approach and then tried to suppress the smile. He spoke to her.

"Why aren't you drinking?" she asked.

"I don't know. It gets me into trouble. I'm not against it or anything."

"Don't say too much. I want a soda."

From there it went on, virtually without interruption. He thought at times that he should tell her all about it—the scarlet sin—but he did not want to and he heard and saw every clue from her that she would not want to hear it.

There was no one like her. She taught English at Beckley College and a children's Sunday School class at First Presbyterian and loved to dance. There was a boyfriend, sort of, at the college, but he was very easy to slip. She said things in passing that amazed him, but there was no trying to be serious and there were no masquerades. Everything was on the surface. He learned that even the depths were on the surface. He learned the jitterbug at the Starlighter and the two-step at the First Presbyterian Church gymnasium and spent more time than he could have ever imagined at plays and recitals on the Beckley College campus. He wondered at the ease of it, but he did not ask why.

On Valentine's day, she did the asking. "My parent's club," she said. "They have a dinner dance thing there. People our age. It'll be fun."

The light through the western windows washed the long ballroom. Not streaming rays, the sun was already behind the mountain. It was ambient light. The last of day. A kind of still presence, posing as Permanence, as if to preserve the perfect moment: the polite crowd, the set tables, the soft clink of fork and knife.

They sat with two other couples, friends of hers from the college. "That's true." She said, and she laughed with the other girls. Her dress was rose, the color of the sunset cloudbreasts above the mountain.

He took his plate to the serving table and she talked to the others, her hands darting like white birds.

For the first time since the divorce, he drank wine. She knew of his resolution, but said nothing. She came with the round stem in her fingers, the rose wine, the misted glass. Now it was evening and the light from the chandeliers caught her hair, her silver bangles, her necklace. Everywhere sparkle. Drink ye of it.

When the music started, she talked of the dancers. She knew the couples. "There," she said. "Watch them."

Her song came later and with the downbeat she took his hand and led him to the dance floor. She was singing.

He was no dancer. She laughed.

When the slow song came, she pressed against him. He stepped and she moved with him.

Weightless. She was light in his arms. Take ye of it.

One of her girlfriends from graduate school got married in North Carolina and they went. It was a big church wedding on a sunny spring day. At the end of the service he said to her, *I think we probably ought to go ahead and do this. Do you need to know anything more about me before we do?*

"Do you know enough about me?"

10

Varner parked his cruiser in the narrow lot behind the Boone County High School gymnasium. It was not yet dawn and Varner sat in the cruiser and drank coffee from a thermal plastic mug. Between drinks he set the mug on the dash. The steam from the coffee fogged a spot on the windshield. He looked around the parking lot. There were a few empty cars, no one moving anywhere. After a time he re-started the engine and adjusted the heater.

At the back of the gymnasium a red-painted metal door opened and a man dressed in a sweatsuit stepped out into the parking lot and jammed a basketball between the top of the door and the door frame and tried the door to make sure it would not fall closed and walked into the parking lot and to Varner's cruiser. Varner opened his door.

"You Varner?"

"Yeah."

"I'm Harless. Deputy Harless."

"You guys already started?"

"We just got it open. We came in from the front. Guys are getting dressed. Come on."

Varner took a rolled towel and a pair of basketball shoes from the passenger seat and took his holstered revolver from underneath his seat. He opened the trunk of the cruiser, laid the revolver on the trunk floor, closed the trunk and followed the man into the gymnasium. The red door opened onto a short hallway where pictures of standing basketball and baseball teams hung, each labeled by year and record. The hallway led to the gym and there were doors to locker rooms on either side of the hall. Varner looked down the hallway and into the gym where there were clusters of men at several of the baskets. He heard the basketballs slapping against the wooden court and their echoes in the large, almost empty gymnasium, a rapid-fire, speed-bag sound.

Harless took the basketball out of the doorway and dribbled the ball as he trotted through the hallway and onto the court. As he passed the locker room doorways he pointed to the right and looked back at Varner.

"We got that one unlocked. You can dress in there."

Varner pushed through the locker room door and walked past a cinderblock privacy partition into the open room. There were a dozen or more men in various stages of dress sitting on the benches in front of the locker rows, standing beside lockers, standing at urinals. One man who stood was in full sheriff's department uniform. He had unbuttoned his shirt and his clip-on tie dangled from an edge of the shirt, doubled over a tie-tack like a dead body across a horse. In front of the deputy a black, patent leather gunbelt was draped across the bench where Jack Sampson sat. He looked at the floor as he pulled on athletic socks. No one acknowledged Varner's entry into the room until a very tall man unbent from tying his shoe. He wore thick, black framed glasses which were secured with an elastic strap. He looked at Varner.

"Hey, Mark. Glad you made it."

The very tall man started to trot toward the door.

"Hey, Johnson." Varner said. "You guys got a reason for starting so early?"

"Only time we can get the gym. Get dressed. Let's go."

IT WAS cold in the locker room and the only sounds were from the lockers as their doors were slammed and as shoes were dropped onto their metal floors. Varner did not again speak, nor was he spoken to until he was on the court shooting warm-ups. He moved into the group of seven men at the basket nearest the hallway where he had entered and stood under the basket without speaking. He nodded occasionally as he tossed back a basketball to a shooter after a made shot. He took his turns shooting. Johnson came from a group under the basket at the opposite end of the gym and over to Varner.

"We got the teams. You're with me and those guys over there."

He pointed to a side basket where only three men stood and began walking back to the opposite end of the court. He continued to speak to Varner who shot the ball in his hands, then followed down the court.

"We got first game. We're shirts. Play to fifteen—point a basket. We'll start with a two-three zone. You're outside. You and Chapman—the red-headed guy over there—bring the ball up the floor."

The knots of shooters cleared out from under the baskets and Varner tossed a ball in-bounds to Chapman who dribbled up the court and across the half-court line. Varner trotted up the other side of the court and to the corner. Johnson moved from underneath the basket to high post at the foul line as Chapman brought the ball into the frontcourt.

As Johnson moved up from the basket, Varner broke from the corner and across the lane. Chapman bounce-passed the ball past his defender into Johnson who, without dribbling, pivoted to the right and hit Varner just outside the lane with another bounce-pass. The low-post defender stepped out of the lane to cover Varner, who was less than ten feet from the basket. Varner pivoted away from the basket and dribbled two steps outside as Johnson broke from the foul line for the basket. Varner pivoted back toward the basket and took the ball into the air, as if attempting a jump-shot. The ball arced from Varner's hand and above the out-stretched arms of the defender and into the grip of Johnson, who was at the top of his jump. Johnson brought the ball back to the court, slammed down a single dribble, then leapt mightily at the basket and shoved the ball over the rim and into the net with the snap and voracity of a dog tearing meat.

As they started back down the court, Johnson trotted up alongside of Varner.

"Very nice," he said. "This one is going to be easy."

It *was* easy. The first game was over quickly with Varner's team winning 15—7. Winner stayed up. The next game was not much closer, Varner, Johnson, Chapman and two very able forwards took this one too–15–10.

After this second game Varner took a long drink from a wall fountain and walked back out onto the court and sat down near the top of the key. He extended his arms behind him, pressed his open hands against the court, leaned back and surveyed the bleachers surrounding the court. There was a line of small windows along the wall above the top bleacher. The glass in those windows was reinforced with wire. Through them Varner could see that it was now daylight. Here and there on the bleachers were a few onlookers, children, wives, girlfriends, older policemen. He took the bottom edge of his T-shirt and wiped the sweat from his face. The next team left the bleachers and began shooting warm-ups at the basket on the opposite end of the court. Jack Sampson was there.

Sampson put a heavy hand in the middle of Varner's back as Varner stood just above the opponent's goal to receive the in-bounds pass from Chapman. This was the first effort of the day at full-court defense. Varner broke to the far side of the court and a forward ran back down court on the near side and took the in-bounds pass and returned it to Chapman, who brought the ball up court.

Sampson kept a hand on Varner down the court and there did not conform to his team's zone defense, but continued to follow Varner all over the court, one-on-one.

The teams traded goals, with neither Sampson nor Varner scoring, until Chapman fired a long jumper to tie the game at 14-14. On the made basket and before Sampson's team had in-bounded the ball, Chapman yelled, "*Win by two.*"

Chapman then turned his back on the in-bounds play and took a few steps down the floor. Then, apparently without reference to anything he should have been able to perceive, he pivoted and broke back and in front of Sampson, who had positioned himself to catch the in-bounds pass. Chapman broke up the pass by tapping the ball across court to Varner, who had seen the play developing and was breaking back to the basket. Varner took the pass in perfect stride and sank an unchallenged layup. Varner's team did not this time turn down the floor. As the ball bounced once, twice, after the made basket, the teams lined up man to man for what the defenders—who now bounced on the balls of their feet, seemingly renewed—hoped would be the last in-bounds play.

A guard from Sampson's team took the ball out-of-bounds and looked for an open man. Varner stood just inside the baseline, nose to nose with the man holding the ball. His arms were flailing. "Come on, man." He yelled. "You got five seconds to get it in."

The guard threw the ball high and long for a team-mate breaking deep down court. The pass was short. Chapman ran under it, intercepted the ball with the intended receiver coming back for the ball and onto Chapman's back. Chapman kept control and, without a dribble, whipped a short pass from mid-court to Varner at the top of the key. Varner saw an opening in the mass of moving bodies and broke full speed for the basket. As he began his jump for the hoop, Sampson, moving crosscourt, ran into the lane and stopped dead in Varner's path. Sampson lifted his right arm and caught Varner with an elbow in the face. Varner dropped to the court like a stone, the back of his head bouncing as it hit the wood.

Varner was bleeding from a cut beneath his eye. Johnson grabbed a towel from a low bleacher and doused it in a drinking fountain and pressed it against the cut.

"You okay, Mark?"

Varner was up on his knees now. He looked at the floor. "Yeah, I'm okay."

"Hey Jimmy," Johnson yelled to an onlooker. "Bring my cruiser around. I'm taking him to the emergency room."

In a few moments, Varner was sitting up on the court. The towel was stained with blood spots the size of tomato slices. Jimmy came back into the gym.

"Let's go," he said.

Johnson knelt and wrapped Varner's arm around his neck. The two then stood up. On the way out of the gym, Johnson glared at Sampson who was sitting on a low bleacher.

"I don't know what in the hell it is with you, man. You've got a real problem."

The game was not restarted. Two other teams left the bleachers and started a new game. Sampson headed for the showers. When he came back into the gym, Tonya Dawson, who was sitting on the first bleacher, smiled at him.

"How about a ride home, honey?" she said.

11

In 1969, the biggest mine in Boone County was ordered closed twice for sub-standard ventilation. Jim Gribble was the man who ordered it closed. He was a big guy and could take the heat which came from every side since the shutdown cost the company over forty thousand dollars in revenue, and each of the 106 employees about sixty dollars in wages for every day it was closed. He got no solace at home, either. "You just like the feelin' it gives you—you bein' the boss of everybody," she said. "You forget people are livin' hand to mouth. We got neighbors that are gonna be doin' without because the mines is closed." But Gribble knew right from wrong. The place was dangerous and his duty was clear. It needed to be closed.

There was one person that sympathized with Jim. She was employed at Catton Number Two on the other side of the county. She had just been transferred in from the main office in Baltimore and worked long hours on some kind of accounting. She was usually the only one left in the field office trailer at the end of the day when Jim usually finished his walkaround inspection at Number Two.

"You're the guy that closed down Amos Number Nine, aren't you?" She smiled as she asked it and quickly added, "Look, I don't hate you. I think human life has some value, too. Even if nobody else in this godforsaken place does."

She was performing an internal audit. "You think you've got it tough, try telling the Neanderthals around here something about how to run a business. Try doing that if you are a woman. I'd love to hear what they say about me."

She was thirty-one, two years older than he, and married to her career. She had an earthy sense of humor, which Jim appreciated—particularly in an intellectual woman. She also kept a bottle of scotch in her desk. She admired him for his resolve, she said. It was that kind of thing that would bring some much needed changes into this unbelievably backward place where little value was placed on human life. She certainly was not backward. Not about sex at any rate. If two people—two adults—agreed on something—if they both knew the score going in, then what was the problem? There would be people who wouldn't understand that, of course. Just like there were people around who didn't understand simple accounting practices and didn't understand why a mine has to be properly ventilated. They definitely had alot in common. They were two enlightened people surrounded by a bunch of brutes who didn't understand them. The comfort Jim Gribble took in her uninhibited affection absolutely sustained him through the ordeal of the closures.

When it became apparent to him that he must order Catton Number Two closed, he was sure she would understand. Although she was a company woman, she would have no patience with her own employer for such an abuse of the employees. He would have to do something for her though, and he was thinking of some way to get some money out of the household accounts in a way his wife would not suspect as he confronted the mine boss with the closure order. He abandoned this train of thought when the mine boss showed him the pictures which his wife and his boss, who were both adults but had not known the score going in, would never understand. His children would not understand them either the mine boss said, and didn't he have a daughter starting school this fall, and what would he do for her without his income?

It was a lesson learned. His job was his own to do. He could and would from now on accept solace from no one. He would not close down Catton. The boss had promised to have the problem fixed within a week, anyway. Perhaps he had been too anxious to order the closure in anticipation of the continued admiration from the woman. Let it go. Let it go and get your ass out of this county. Inspectors are transferred all the time. All he had to do was ask. He would start over.

On November 21, 1969, the Number Two Catton mine at Heart Creek in Boone County blew up. A later investigation revealed that the ventilation system for the mine was sub-standard, but had not been reported by the MSHA inspector who had accepted favors from a whore provided him by Catton Coal Company. In that explosion, which claimed a total of thirty-two lives, a railcar that had been used to transport miners from the mouth of the mine to the coal face was shot from the mouth of the mine, across a ravine and into a sheer sandstone cliff on the other side. It was like an industrial size and strength Evel Knevil launch. Of course, all six men aboard were undoubtedly killed immediately by the concussion from the blast.

IN NOVEMBER of 1969 Jack Sampson was eighteen years old. It was the year that he, a senior fullback, carried Seth High School to the state single-A championship game. In the semi-finals, he carried the ball for 191 yards and three touchdowns. Seth led Harper High 33—0 late in the fourth quarter when Jeff Simms, Harper's 145 pound free safety, intercepted a pass deep in his own territory. The sophomore, hoping to avoid a complete shutout, shifted his field and headed up the sidelines. He was at full tilt when Sampson and Boyd Potts, a 220 pound lineman, executed a well-planned clothesline tackle on him. Potts hit the kid low, Sampson high. The sound of Simms' fibula cracking was audible in the stands.

Coach Clark knew football was a rough game. He knew that every time he put the Seth team on the field, there was a substantial chance someone would get hurt—sometimes very badly hurt. He also knew that football was a young man's game. It was a game that, at the high school level at least, was played under the influence of runaway testosterone. That was the game. You went balls out. Everybody understood that.

But there were limits. The heat of passion was one thing; in football it is an absolute defense. Premeditation was another: there was never an excuse for any player calculating to injure another. Another thing was the lopsided score. Everyone on the field knew the game was already over. There was no justification for it. The sight of the ambulance wheeling onto the field against the backdrop of that scoreboard showing a minute and fourteen seconds left to play made Coach Clark sick at his stomach. A coach should only tolerate so much, he thought. He walked onto the field and, before the standing-room-only crowd, yanked his two star seniors, sending them to the locker room.

It was not unusual for Coach Clark to be late getting to the bus after a game. Very often there were words that had to be spoken in the aftermath: praise for heroic but unnoticed performances, encouragement for an underclassman who had dropped an all-important pass, and sometimes a word of discipline. The players and the coaching staff knew these sessions were absolutely private. There was a face and a voice the coach showed the group. What went on in the after-game sessions was not for the group. Everybody on the bus knew that. Everyone there knew that the three people absent from their ranks—Potts, Sampson, and Coach Clark were not to be disturbed. That knowledge preserved the coach's privacy for over an hour after the game and may have preserved it longer had it not been unseasonably cold that night and had the team not had a two hour drive ahead of them. It was twenty minutes until midnight when Phil Ferrell, the line coach, tapped a student-manager on the shoulder. "Why don't you walk over there and see if we've left any equipment around or anything?"—meaning go see if you can get the story and be careful about it.

The job did not require stealth. The manager could hear the voices as he approached the fieldhouse. They rose and fell, allowing him to hear only parts of the argument. He quickly made out that there were two sides—the coach and Potts were arguing, if not pleading, with Sampson. The issue was whether Sampson would stay on the team to play in the state championship game the next week. What the kid remembered and what he would repeat time and again in locker rooms, and later bar rooms, was the last pitch the coach made to his star senior. The coach spoke loudly, evenly, and with an air of finality: "Jack, you'll be sorry for this. Next Friday is far more important to you than this little spat with me. You may not realize that right now, but you will realize it soon. I just hope you have the sense to realize that before it's too late."

Those words did not have the effect the coach had hoped for, but Jack Sampson never forgot them. Had he played the game, his father would have traveled to Parkersburg on Friday. He would have been at the wheel of his 1965 half-ton pickup truck at the time the Catton Number Two mine exploded and not in the railcar that was shot from its mouth like a rocket-sled.

COAL MINING is a dangerous business. There is nothing abstract about it. It is as unforgiving as gravity and as subtle as steel against stone. It is done for money, and the success or failure of a coal mine is determined on a balance sheet. There are economic problems that can halt a coal operation or render it unprofitable. The loss of a few or even several miners in an accident is not one of them. When the simple laws of supply and demand are allowed to apply unchecked in a mining context, labor is a very cheap item. After all, the biggest qualification for a miner was the willingness to take the unreasonable risks incident to the job. The economic term for such relatively unskilled labor was "fungible," meaning one miner was just the same as another.

Thus, the union.

A labor union, like any other organization, must have a theory. It must have a reason for being. It is not merely a response to another entity. If it is to have a life, it must have a set of ideas. The ideas that support other organizations have established sources. Churches have seminaries, businesses and governments have universities. In all of these cases, the undergirding doctrines, have been thought out, recorded, analyzed, restated, studied, and applied. A churchman is a seminarian, a politician is a lawyer or a student of some other social science. Both are students in the classic sense of the term. There is no contradiction between being highly educated and being a leader in any of these fields. With the union, it is different. The important doctrine in a labor union cannot be taught in a classroom. It cannot be articulated. It cannot be absorbed vicariously. It can only be held by the heart. A formally educated labor leader is like a white civil rights leader: he may have great sympathy for the movement, his motives may be pure, but he is not baptized, he cannot really *know*.

12

Varner picked up his pace as he turned the corner at the bottom of the hill and began the last leg of his run—up the hill to the barracks. Because of the heat he had waited until after sunset to run and as he came over the first rise in the long hill, the quonset hut barracks were only a grey outline against the dark forested hillside. Just above the ridge in the eastern sky a low line of the evening's first stars stretched, faint and muted in the summer haze.

Sweat fell in large drops from the points of his elbows as his arms swung in the rhythm of his stride. He crossed into the cinder lot of the barracks. On the front stoop of the quonset he leaned forward and with his outstretched hands braced himself against the door. He took a half step back and held himself at that angle, pushing his heels against the porch floor until he felt his calves and thigh muscles relax. He went inside, dripping sweat down the hallway and stopped at a Bank of Danville wall calendar, and on the square for September 6th he wrote "4M—34:26, hills, hot."

He walked slowly into the bathroom and turned on the faucet and drank from his cupped hands and then rubbed handfuls of cool water on his face. He dried his face, moving the towel gently over the bruise around his right eye. He hung the towel over his neck and went into the kitchen. He saw through the back window that nothing was left of twilight, and that there was a car idling with its lights off in the lot behind the barracks. He went to the bunk room and in the near-darkness put on a nylon running jacket, tucked his service revolver into a zippered pocket of the jacket and went out the front door of the barracks. Near the corner of the quonset he went to his hands and knees in the cinders, then to his belly and forearms and worked his way to the edge of the hut. For a few minutes he looked back at the rear of the idling car, then he stood up, went back through the front door and to the kitchen and flipped a panel of switches. The kitchen lights came on and a streetlight above the rear lot came flickering on. He went out the back door and walked toward the car.

When Varner stepped off of the back stoop and out of the shadow, the car engine stopped and the driver opened the door. The light from the opened door triangulated away across the cinder lot. The driver stood up behind the open door, resting his left forearm on the door top.

"Hey, R. L.," Varner yelled.

"Hidey, Mark. I didn't know you was back yet. I thought you'd of had a light on."

"I just got back a minute ago. I was washing off. You must have driven in right behind me."

Varner continued toward the car until he stood just on the other side of the opened car door. He watched

R.L. Maddux look at him at such an angle and for such a length of time so that he knew Maddux was inspecting his bruise, but Maddux made no comment and Varner gave no sign of knowing.

"You want to come in?"

"Thank you. I can't right now. I only got a minute."

Maddux was still as he looked across the roof of his car toward the road. A coal truck strained up the hillside, downshifting as it neared the barracks. The noise from the truck blared, then faded. Maddux continued to stare toward the road.

"You need to know something," Maddux said.

"I know."

"No. I mean you need to know something you don't even know you need to know."

"I might surprise you."

"You know you're playing with far?" Maddux asked.

"Yeah."

"I don't mean just the case. That, too. But there's more than that."

"You mean Sampson?"

Maddux shook his head. "Nah. I don't mean Sampson. I mean that girl. You're dealing with a crazy woman."

"I know," Varner said again.

"You don't know *how* crazy. You don't have no idea."

"I might have some idea. What can you tell me?"

"She started out trying to be crazy. Acting like she was crazy on purpose. Doing things with drugs. Now there's times she can't help it. She is as crazy as she used to act like she was. I've found her on the street at night and she says she doesn't know me. She gives me other names and she believes it."

"That's our business, R.L.," said Varner. "Dealing with crazy people."

"I'm tellin' you. You'll go a long time without meeting one like her. She will hurt you. She will find a way."

"What are you telling me?"

"I'm telling you to watch out. You watch out around her."

"I've got to watch out around everybody. That's nothing new."

"Yes, it is," Maddux raised his voice. "It is something new. She's different."

"You think she might know anything?"

"I'm sure she does."

"How are you sure?"

Maddux paused and shifted his weight. "You get to where you just know things after awhile. When things happen, you know, in a little place like this, there's only so many people who could've done them. Only so many people who would know. I know who lives under almost every roof on this side of the county. I know them in a way other than people usually say they know each other. You do this job long enough and keep your eyes open and watch what happens and if you can keep your distance you get to know people real good. You don't have no illusions about them. If you would write down just exactly what happens, nobody would believe it."

"Then tell me who killed Helton."

Maddux shook his head slowly and again looked away from Varner and across the top of the car and to the road.

"I don't know that."

"But, she knows? You think she knows?"

"No. I don't mean that she knows exactly who did it. But, she'll know something. She will have heard things that we haven't heard. It may be all wrong, but it would get you started. You'd at least find out what people are really saying about it."

"I think that's right."

"But you're crazy to deal with her alone. She'll burn you."

"You want in."

"I *am* in. This is my county. It's my job to solve that murder as much as it is yours."

"You want to work her with me, I mean."

"I'm offerin'."

"I don't know, R.L. I don't know. I don't know lots of things about this place. What is the deal with your buddy, Sampson? What do you know about him?"

"I know everything there is to know about him. I know him better than anybody else does."

"He in on this?"

"No."

"What in the hell is with him?"

"It's a long story."

"I need to hear it."

"Maybe you do. But, I don't have time to tell it to you tonight. You come to my house tomorrow. I'll cook you dinner. You got to be tired of eatin' your own cookin'."

Varner smiled. "You do know people," he said.

13

Varner was farther up this river road than he had ever been. He was far past the last intersection, where this road led to another road, and the road was narrow now, so narrow that the last car he met coming the other direction had pulled onto a wide, flat place and allowed Varner to pass. Every now and then he still passed a house or a cleared field with a driveway leading to the road, but now most of it was woods. The road went from two lanes to one, then from blacktop to gravel, then petered out into a set of ruts through a pasture, ending at a long row of tall hemlocks.

Varner pulled the car into the pasture and left it there and walked on stepping stones through an arch cut through the interlaced branches of the hemlocks and out onto a new-cut lawn as broad and long as a pasture. The lawn sloped away from Varner and down to a white frame house on the riverbank. Large trees were here and there on the lawn—massive white oaks with low branches stretching away knotted and bent like muscled arms with great pools of shade beneath them and tall poplars with branchless trunks straight and thick like the columns of some ancient city. The land was drinking in its last draught of summer, the grass and the trees gilded with the strong light and the soil and the river baking and setting free the scents of the earth—the mineral smells from the opened pores of the damp river rocks and the smell of new cut grass and the rarest hint from the virgin hemlocks—the bitter, clean and astringent scent of those dark and untamed things whose ancestors grew here in the very shadows of the glaciers.

The house stood beneath two of the largest oaks. It was completely shaded, and surrounded by a low, covered porch. A swing hung from a corner of the porch ceiling and there hung also a few potted plants and vines. To the far side of the house and out of the shade, there was a vegetable garden on a terrace at the top of the riverbank. Maddux stood in the garden, working a potato fork. He wore a wide brimmed straw hat and a white, long-sleeved shirt. When he saw Varner he stopped and with a wide wave of his arm signaled Varner to come across to the garden.

Varner walked across the lawn in the shade in front of the house and underneath a rose trellis, and as he came toward the garden the soil grew softer, like moss under his footsteps.

As he stepped up the rise to the top of the riverbank and the garden terrace, he could see into the garden and the half-row of dull red potatoes that lay exposed in Maddux's wake. The soil of the newly turned row was black against the sunbleached surface of the garden and as Varner walked onto the terrace he walked into the damp and clean smell of the broken earth.

The men said their greetings and Varner said that the place was beautiful and not what he had imagined and like nothing else he had seen in that county. Maddux said that the place had been in his wife's family for three generations before them, and that it was an unusual tract of land for Boone County in that the mineral rights to the land had never been sold. Most of the mineral rights had been severed from the surface rights over seventy years ago, Maddux said. His wife's great-grandfather had been a rebel soldier who had come to this county from Wise County, Virginia with what was left of a family fortune. He wanted to start a farm and orchard. He saw before he died that the mines were coming and that the Yankees from up north were coming for the land, and he fixed a provision in his will which prevented the severance of the mineral rights from the land for the life of his last then-living heir, plus 21 years. His last heir, Maddux's wife's mother, had died in 1973.

As Maddux told the story, he continued to push the tines of the garden fork into the raised row and sift fist-sized potatoes from the soil.

"That's enough potatoes, don't you think?" said Varner.

"They ain't as much as they look now once they's cleaned and peeled and fried up."

"Come on, R.L., that's got to be twenty potatoes. I never eat more than ten, myself, even if they are small. I make that a rule."

"I don't aim to eat 'em all at once. You might want to take a few back to the barracks with you. They keep good. All winter. Go over to that shed and take a peck basket off the back wall and get these up. Pull up some of them onions over there and a few of them green peppers, too."

Varner lifted a small basket off of a nail on the side of the outbuilding. He set it beside the garden, grabbed an onion stalk at the base and worked it gently. As the garden surface cracked around it and gave way, he pulled from the ground a yellow onion the size of a baseball. Holding the stalk, he knocked the head of the onion against an open hand a few times, rubbed his thumb over a cake of dirt clinging to its underside, then dropped the onion into the basket.

"Pull a dozen. I like 'em half and half. Half taters and half onions. They won't be wasted."

Varner went to his knees beside the row of onions and pulled eleven more, dropping them into the basket as he went. Then he stood up and took the basket in hand and spoke to Maddux.

"This is enough for an army."

Maddux turned back on the row he had finished and with the sharp end of the middle tine of the potato fork cut the potatoes, one by one, from their vines. He carried the fork back to the shed, hung it on the wall, then took a burlap sack from the ground and dropped the potatoes into it.

"Let's go on in."

Varner and Maddux walked side-by-side along the garden terrace, down a bank to the lawn and the house and onto the porch. A grey-haired woman, dressed in loose fitting clothing, appeared in the open doorway. In one hand she carried a couple of thick and worn paperback novels and in the other a wide ring of keys.

"I want you to meet my girlfriend," said Maddux.

The woman smiled at Varner.

"This is Lucy, my first wife."

"Nice to meet you, Mrs. Maddux."

"Nice to meet you, Mark."

She then spoke to her husband. "I'm goin' over to Carolyn's. There's tea in the refrigerator and the coffee maker is set. Don't save me any dinner."

"You don't know what you're missing, honey. I'm frying potatoes."

"I know what I'm missing. You boys have a good time."

The kitchen was at the back of the house and opened onto a kind of sun porch that had been added on, though not recently. The row of windows in the back wall of the porch allowed a view of the river, which looked still and green and shimmery in the afternoon sun. Maddux did not turn on any lights in the kitchen, but lit a stove burner and laid several strips of bacon in a skillet and set the skillet on the low fire. He moved a floor fan from another room into the sun porch and pointed it so as to draw air from the kitchen and blow it through the rear screen door. The big fan blade whispered loudly and the bacon began to sizzle in the skillet. Maddux dropped a dozen or so potatoes and several onions into one side of a double sink, took a peeler from a drainer and turned on a cold, medium stream of water and began peeling. Having done three or so potatoes, he laid the tool aside and wiped his hands on a towel hanging from the oven handle, moved a step away from the sink and laid a cutting board on the counter.

"You peel the rest of these and skin these onions. I'm going to cut these up and get them in the skillet. That grease is good and hot."

Varner stepped in front of the sink and started on a potato while Maddux diced the potatoes he had already peeled, then took the laden cutting board in hand and turned to the stove. With the big knife he scraped the mound of diced potatoes into the hot skillet and it sizzled loudly as a cloud of steam rose off the skillet.

"Get me an onion. Maddux stirred the skillet with the big knife. I need an onion right now."

Varner got through a couple of the onions quickly and just as quickly they were diced and into the mix in the skillet and the kitchen was filled with the smell of the fresh, sweet roots and the pepper and spices Maddux shook onto them as they browned. Maddux turned the potatoes a few times with the knife until their insides were soft to the knife and a fine crust had started to form. Then he poured vinegar into his cupped hand, held it over the skillet, made a fist and sprinkled the vinegar over the mix. He turned off the fire and covered the skillet with a flat lid. The smell of the vinegar and the browned onions and peppers and bacon and pepper was strong and full, and as Varner leaned against the counter in the kitchen his mouth watered till his throat ached, and then he heard a trickle of new coffee filling the glass pot and that warm and familiar smell settled him and he relaxed and waited.

Maddux pulled plates from a cabinet and, with the knife, scraped potatoes onto the plates. He took a couple of tomatoes from the counter, sliced them then laid the slices on another plate and got coffee and glasses of iced water. The men carried the whole mess into the sun porch and laid it on the table and sat down. There was an embroidered cloth over the table and the draw of the fan rustled its edge. Varner did not begin to eat, but looked at Maddux and did not speak. Maddux smiled, closed his eyes and returned thanks for the food.

Varner tried the potatoes and they were hot and salty and spicy and crisp and he tasted the bacon and the peppers and onions in the crust and took a long draught from the glass of iced water and a drink of the hot coffee.

"You're a good cook, R.L.. This water even tastes good."

"It's out of the spring over across the hill. Best water in all of Boone County, right there. It's in the coffee, too."

The tomatoes were blood red and soft and tart as citrus and Varner salted them heavily and ate slice after slice.

"Beats eatin' at the barracks, I bet." Maddux said.

"Beats about anything."

"They's more in the skillet. Still hot."

Varner loaded his plate again and warmed up his coffee from the glass pot and sat again and drank the hot coffee which seemed to invigorate his palate and sharpen the entire experience. Maddux's plate was clean and he took it and his cup back to the kitchen and returned with his cup full again and a lit cigar.

"I didn't figure it was any use askin' you about a seegar."

"You figured right. They don't bother me, though. You go right ahead."

Varner pushed away his plate and sat back in the chair. His hands were resting on the table and he began to reach for his coffee but returned his hand to rest and looked out the window at the warm, bright afternoon and then looked up to the ceiling and drew a long breath and closed his eyes. Maddux pulled slowly on the cigar and the droning fan drew away the smoke and the still afternoon was golden and all was silent for a time.

"You was wanting to know about Sampson." Maddux said.

"I'm sorry, R.L.," Varner opened his eyes. "What did you say?"

"You was wanting to know about Jack Sampson."

"Yeah."

"You ever hear of Curtis Johnson?"

"The football player?"

"Yeah. He's from Boone County. Did you know that?"

"I knew he was from somewhere down here," Varner said. "I knew he was from in state."

"You follow his career much?"

"Football's not really my game. I remember when he was at WVU. I got tired of hearing about him. I know he's with the Oilers, or was."

"Still is. He was all-pro again last year."

Varner held his cup in both hands and tapped the bottom against the tabletop. He nodded.

"You know who holds the high school rushing records in this county?"

"Him, I guess."

"He holds one. He holds it for most yardage in a game, single game. You know who holds the records for total career, total season and average yards per carry?"

"Got me." Varner shrugged.

"Jack Sampson."

"Okay. I'm still listening. That was a long time ago."

"It was sixty-seven through sixty-nine."

"You must be a real fan."

Maddux tapped the ash from his cigar into a spitoon at his feet.

"I haven't been to a game in years. We all have our seasons, though."

"Those were your seasons?"

"In a way. I knew Jack's daddy. Worked with him in the mines. He was killed in an explosion over at Glady during Jack's senior year."

Varner did not respond.

"He was a good man. One of the worst strikes we ever had around here was in sixty-nine. It started in the winter and wasn't over 'til plumb over into October. Blue-Jay put up a fifteen-foot high fence around the entrance to the mines. They's bob-wire strung all along the top of it. Back then Blue-Jay's offices and showers was right there at the drift-mouth—all of it right across the road from a little camp called Gripp.

"Just a few old company houses is all it was by then. Anyway, the company kept a pack of dogs behind that fence to keep the picketers out. Five Dobermans. Kept 'em hungry. One morning a guard forgot to close a gate and the first person to walk by it was the preacher's seven-year-old girl on her way to school. Her mommy was a-watchin' her from the living room window. She says she saw them black dogs a-comin' down the hillside and through the gate as fast and as quiet as the wind. She was so scared she couldn't move. Them dogs knocked the little girl down and started rippin' and tearin' at her.

"Next thing the mommy saw was Jack. He took a runnin' kick at one dog—right under its chin. Sent it into the air whinin' and a-spittin' blood. Two of the other dogs ran off, but two of 'em wouldn't turn loose a' the little girl. The mommy said she saw Jack reach down and grab them dogs—one with each hand—around the necks like that." Maddux extended his arms, holding his thumbs and fingers in rigid 'C' shapes, shaking them for emphasis. "She said when Jack grabbed the dogs his back was toward her and she was lookin at the backs of the dogs and could see the dogs jerk their heads up bug-eyed away from the girl and their noses up into the air and show their teeth and bend their legs trying to push back away and then one of the dogs laid down and then the other. When they looked at the dogs they saw their windpipes had been crushed. Jack snapped them dogs' necks with his hands."

Varner took his empty cup into the kitchen and took the glass pot out of the coffeemaker and found that the half-inch of coffee left was cold. He poured the coffee out into the sink and rinsed the pot and set it upside down on a drain-board in the other well of the sink. He stood at the sink and turned to his left and stared out the side window. He combed an open hand back through his hair. When he returned to the table, Maddux still sat there, still with his cigar.

"Where does it go from there?" Varner asked.

"Downhill, mostly. I don't think he ever got over his dad's death. He made the team down at Marshall, got hurt, wasn't on the plane when it crashed."

"*The* Marshall plane crash?"

"Yeah. Jack had gotten hurt and didn't make the trip for that game."

"My God."

"Anyway, he ended up in Vietnam, got a medal or two there, came back, worked in the mines, was active in the Union, then took the job he has now."

"That had to be a big pay cut. Why did he leave the mines?"

"That's what I don't know."

"When did he leave the mines?"

"Four years ago."

"You don't have any idea why?"

"I've asked him," Maddux said. "He hasn't told me the truth."

"But, why do you think?"

"There's lots of good reasons to get out from under-ground. It's dangerous and it's depressin' work."

"But you don't think it's either of those?"

"His mother didn't want him in the mines, but I don't think that's it."

"He married?"

"No."

"Ever been?"

"No."

"Where are the women?"

"I don't know. He goes into Charleston pretty regu-lar. I don't talk to him about that."

"How long was he in the mines?"

"Seventy-two to eighty-eight. Sixteen years.""

"What about Tonya Dawson? Anything between her and Sampson?"

"No. I'd know if there was."

"What about her husband, Sam? Anything between him and Sampson?"

"They were union brothers."

"Tonya says Sam killed Helton," Varner said.

"I don't know. They're both union."

"She says it was for other reasons."

"Drugs?"

"Yeah."

"They *are* into dope."

"How big?"

"Bigger than you'd think. They grow it."

"How much?"

"I don't know exactly how much. They grow it all through these hollers. There are out-of-state people in and out of here dealin' in it. There's more stuff goin' on than anybody imagines. There are killings in this county that never make the papers. I believe that." Maddux drew on what was left of his cigar. "What does she say happened?" he said.

"Says Helton owed Sam for a shipment. Says that Sam's guy leaned on him hard for the money and Sam had to do it."

"That ain't it."

"I know."

"Helton grows it. He wouldn't have been buying anything from Sam Dawson. That is real interesting, though. Why would she be sayin' that?" Maddux dropped the stub of his cigar into the spittoon. He stood. "Will you drink more coffee if I make it?"

14

Mark Varner's normal pace was about seven and a half minutes a mile. Not exactly record breaking, but fast enough to put him among the top over-thirty runners in the department. As he trotted off of the barracks lot, he felt the familiar stiffness in his legs and an overall sluggishness that he knew would soon fade. The first mile was always the slowest. The trick was to think about something else until he hit stride.

Could it be a simple drug murder? Varner pictured the photographs of the scene. Helton had been shot through the front storm door of his trailer—one .357 slug through the forehead. Ballistics said that the shot was point-blank, probably fired through the glass from the front stoop. The living room and one of the bedrooms of the trailer had been ransacked. The closets had been emptied and furniture and clothing thrown onto the floors of those rooms. But the other two bedrooms were untouched; the beds were made. Seventy-four dollars and eighty-nine cents in cash was left on the dresser in the back bedroom.

Varner reached the bottom of the hill and dropped his stride to a comfortable lope. He was not even half a mile out yet and it was no time to begin to strain. Besides, tonight's run might be longer than the regular three and a half mile loop. It was seven-thirty and still broad daylight and hot and humid. Already his shirt was wet enough to cling to him

What did it mean? There was general agreement within the department that the shot through the storm door suggested both familiarity and surprise. It appeared that Helton, who lived alone, had opened the main door of his trailer to a caller on his front porch. One of the forensics people had said that Helton was not only unarmed at the time he was shot, he was disarmed. That is, Helton recognized his assailant and was not alarmed by his presence on his front porch that evening. It appeared he was preparing to open the storm door when he was killed.

Varner sprinted now, gathering speed for the short but steep bank that led up to the swinging bridge. As he left the pavement for the muddy path, his bare legs brushed against clumps of ragweed and stinging nettles that had survived a month of morning frost. Nettle spines caught his shins and thighs and left patches of his now salty skin burning. He ran up the three sandstone steps and onto the wooden deck of the old bridge. His footfalls were loud on the loose planks. Two months ago he wouldn't have set foot on the rickety-looking structure. The other side of the river marked one mile. He felt strong—nearly unconscious of an effort which two years ago, when he was still a smoker, he would have been absolutely incapable.

So what did it mean? Helton had been killed by an acquaintance, and had died without a struggle. The two ransacked rooms meant the killer had been looking for something. The two rooms that were left alone meant that, whatever it was, the killer had found it and left. Mark Varner did not have the answer, but now at least he had two important questions that could certainly be answered: was John Helton a doper; and had drugs or drug paraphernalia been found in his trailer and removed?

Varner picked up the pace. Five miles would come easy tonight.

After showering, Varner pulled the file and opened it on one of the grey metal desks. Helton's rap sheet showed six arrests: Disturbing the Peace, 7/23/84; Resisting Arrest, 7/23/84; Disturbing the Peace, 7/30/84; Contempt of Court, 7/30/84. An attached newspaper clipping explained these charges. Helton had been part of a picket line that had blocked a Norfolk and Western Railroad side track leading away from a non-union mine. The picketers had brawled with troopers at the first confrontation. The company had gotten an injunction. Then, when the leaders were released from jail, they blocked the track again—in defiance of the court's order. Varner raised his eyebrows and shook his head as he viewed the last column. None of the charges had been prosecuted. Lacy Maze, the current Boone County prosecutor, who had twice been involuntarily committed to the county mental hospital, explained part of that, but the contempt of court charge was federal.

The next two charges were from Horry County, South Carolina—Myrtle Beach: Reckless Driving, 7/15/89; Possession of Marijuana, 7/15/89. There it was.

Varner shuffled the file till he found the inventory of Helton's trailer. He flipped the report to the last page: "CONTRABAND: cocaine (white powder)—16 gr.; marijuana (sensimilla—packaged in 13 clear plastic baggies)—13 lbs.," then back to the front page: "OFFICER PERFORMING INVENTORY: Daniel G. Pauley, Deputy, Boone County Sheriff's Office." Varner chuckled. As usual, he would have to go to the courthouse to talk with the deputy. This time, however, he would have to go during visiting hours—Deputy Pauley was in jail.

15

The Boone County Jail was different from many others in that it had, within the last two years, hosted members from each of the three constitutional branches of county government: legislative, executive, and judicial. In all, over twenty percent of the county's elected officials had taken their meals free there during that time. But in many ways it was the same as any fifty-year-old rural county prison. For one thing, as Corporal Varner noticed as he was buzzed through the door, it smelled the same—the same heavy smells of disinfectant, urine, stale cigarette smoke, and vegetable beef soup hung in its hallways.

"Corporal Varner to see inmate Pauley," Varner said to the jailer sitting behind the bulletproof glass.

"Yep. He's on his way down. Just go on in to one of them attorney booths. We'll bring him back there when he gets down."

"Where's the sign?" Varner asked.

"What sign?"

"You know—that big red sign that was right over there on that wall—'If you can't pull the time, then don't pull the crime'. You can still see where it was. The paint's not as dull there."

"We took it down. It was degradin' and dehumanizin'."

Varner knew a company line when he heard one. Now he knew the real answer. He just wanted to hear the deputy say it.

"I kind of liked that sign. Thought it was kind of poetic. The thing must've been up there at least ten years. What brought on the change?"

The deputy did not look up as he replied, "Nothin' particular I know of."

"When did it come down, then?"

"Oh, I reckon about two year ago."

"When did the sheriff start serving his time?"

The deputy continued to stare at a clipboard of papers on his desk. "I don't know," he said. "It was along about then, I reckon."

If any of the same deference had been given former Deputy Daniel G. Pauley, it was not apparent now. The jailer gave no indication that he even knew the former officer as he escorted the pockmarked former deputy across the intake room and into a little stall behind a canvas curtain. Varner was also a little surprised at the former deputy's apparent lack of embarrassment as he faced him through the wire mesh screen in the booth. Pauley gave him the same look most other prisoners did in an interview. It was a hollow look—somewhere between despair and defiance—and seemed to convey the message: *You may have me where you want me, but I have all day and very little to lose.* Varner took the folded inventory report from his jacket pocket, pressed it flat on the counter and pushed it under the screen to the prisoner.

"Need to talk to you about this."

Pauley studied the report for a moment, then looked up at Varner and nodded his head. He looked directly at Varner.

"I remember this one," he said. "What do you need to know?"

"Where did you find the cocaine? Which room was it in?"

"It was in the living room. Ain't that in the report?"

The inmate lifted the top page of the stapled report, looked the next page up and down, then returned to the top page.

"I guess it ain't," he said.

"Where in the living room?" Varner asked.

"Laying on a couch cushion. All the furniture and stuff was in the floor. It was just laying there as white as could be on top of that dark green couch cushion. First thing you saw when you walked in there—besides the body, of course."

"How about the marijuana?"

"That was in the back bedroom—one of the rooms that hadn't been messed up. It was in the closet in a cardboard box. The lid was open."

"Did you know Helton?"

"Yeah. I knew the bastard. Known him all my life."

"Didn't care for him, did you?"

"I liked him okay when he was a kid. His family was dirt poor—lived over there in the holler just above Mink Shoals. He was one lousy adult, though. Those union people—not the locals, now—a bunch of them that came down here from Pennsylvania. They came down in about seventy-seven or so and got ahold of Johnny. That's when his problems with the law started."

"Who do you think killed him?"

"I don't know. Probably some company thug. Live by the sword, die by the sword. Ain't that the way it works?"

"What about the dope? Could it have been drug related?"

"I don't think so, Corporal. For the same reasons you don't. Too much dope left in the house. That's not alot of cocaine, but I've never seen a druggie that will leave a pinch of that stuff lay—and that grass was over five-thousand dollars street value."

16

That evening Varner ran his course around Bandy again. It was seven o'clock and dark night when he opened a small, zippered pocket in his running jacket and took out a key and unlocked the back door to the barracks. He walked straight to the kitchen and turned on the faucet over the sink and cupped his hands together and, with the water still running into them, lowered his head and drank from his cupped hands.

When he had finished drinking, he closed his eyes and splashed the double handful of water onto his face, rubbing with his hands. He turned off the water and walked down the hall toward the shower and when he turned to go into the bathroom and before he had found the light switch he saw movement in the dark room. He jerked away from the bathroom doorway and pulled his revolver from a shoulder holster under his jacket.

"Hey, Mark. Don't be so scared. I'm not gonna hurt you."

Varner stood at the end of the hallway and stared at Tonya Dawson. He was trembling. He pointed the gun to the floor and continued to stare at her. He did not speak. He bent his upper lip in and chewed at his moustache with his front teeth and did not otherwise move.

"How'd you get in?"

"Girls don't tell. We got ways."

"Who else is in here? Tell me now. Who else is here, Tonya?"

"Nobody. I don't want nobody here but you and me. That's more fun."

Her skirt was short and tight and she took little steps toward him down the hall. With both her hands she gathered her hair and pulled it behind her head as she came forward.

"You are so skittish, Trooper Varner," she said. "Like a little pup. I got something here that'll calm you right down."

She reached into a blouse pocket and drew something out and held her hand open to Varner.

"What kind of dope are you doing now? What's that stuff?"

"See, you always think the worst of me. Just like a cop."

She put her hands against his chest and raised her right knee against the inside of his left thigh.

"This ain't dope," she said. "It's candy. M&Ms. Just the green ones. They're afro-deezeeacs. Eat one." She pinched one of the candies and pushed it to his face.

"No, thanks. Had a little something to drink, Tonya?" Varner backed away.

"It's none of your damn business. Anyway, you ought to try a little something yourself, sometime.

Might keep you from being so prissy. You better pat me down, trooper," she giggled. "I could be loaded."

Varner took another step away and did not respond.

"Who do you think you're fooling? You think I don't know you want this? What's the problem?" Tonya demanded. "We already got one dirty little secret between us. What's another one or two? Huh? What's the diff?"

"You don't get it. The secret we have isn't dirty, it's work."

"It's dirty work, then. I'm ratting out my husband to you." She spoke faster. "The daddy of my baby boy is going to spend his life in jail because of this. I'm lying to the man right and left to catch him in a snare for you. Ain't that dirty enough for you?"

"It's not dirty for me."

"Oh, it's okay for you, huh? *My* part is dirty, but *you're* clean? *It's just dirty*, you self-righteous pig." By now she was screaming. "Anybody who touches it gets dirty. I don't care who's got a badge. I don't care what you say the rules are."

"We got no business here tonight, Tonya." Varner slowly shook his head. "You go home."

Tonya did not move. When she spoke it was again in soft voice. She smiled. "See, that's one of your big failings as a cop, Mark. You say things you don't know to be true. We *got* business. I got him on tape."

"You got the tape here?"

"I might."

"This is going no further unless the tape is here."

"I can get it here. Tonight." She brushed back her hair with her fingers, elbows up and out and stepped back toward Varner. "You gonna help a little girl out, Trooper? Don't even tell me you never done it before."

Varner went to the kitchen counter, pulled out a drawer and took out a pencil and pad. He laid the pad on the table and motioned for Tonya to come near. He wrote on the paper. **IS ANYONE ELSE HERE?**

Tonya Dawson smiled, then laughed. When she spoke, she whispered. "No. Just us. She took his hand. Just you and me."

"Show me."

Tonya Dawson was smiling and she held his hand in both of hers and stood on her tiptoes, bouncing. "I just knew you were a whore," she said.

Varner held his revolver in his right hand as she led him by his left through each of the rooms in the barracks. Entering each room, she switched on the light and sang to the tune of the famous passage in Beethoven's Fifth: *Nobody here.*

Varner led her back into the kitchen. "How strange do you like it?" he asked.

"I can do strange. I want everything."

"I got this thing you should know about. I don't like to kiss, Tonya. You kiss me and it's over."

"No kisses."

He led her to the bunkroom and sat her on the bottom bunk. She unbuttoned and removed her blouse and unfastened her bra. He pulled two sets of handcuffs from a drawer and she laughed as he fastened her hands to the posts of the bunk.

"I'll do all the rest," he said.

"Do it, do it, do it."

"This game is called mystery man. You like a little mystery in life, don't you?"

"I like everything. Do it to me."

"What you need to do to make this work is think that you don't know who's with you. I've got to take a shower. I'm dripping sweat. It'll work better this way, anyhow. I'll bet it will be the craziest thing you've..."

"It'll have to go some for that, but try."

Varner slipped the pillowcase from the top bunk and folded it and tied it around her face as a blindfold and left the room. He went to the office room and took a hand-sized recorder from a drawer and pushed a button and held the machine to the light. Then he pushed another button and slapped the machine with his other hand. Then he removed a very small cassette from the machine and held it up to the light and turned it around and put it back into the machine. Again he pushed the button, then held the front of the machine to the light. He dropped the machine back into the drawer and closed the drawer.

Varner took the receiver from the phone on the desk and punched a seven digit number. He spoke in whispers.

"Mrs. Maddux? I'm sorry to be calling so late, but may I please speak to R. L.?"

Varner held the receiver with a shrugged shoulder and closed his eyes and waited.

"R.L.? Great. I've got a real strange favor to ask you, partner. I can't explain everything right now. It's too complicated. I need you to stay on the line here and listen. I'm going to lay this phone down in a room. She won't know it's there. Take good notes and note the time, beginning and end. I'm at the barracks. I'll tell you all about it tomorrow. She says she has a tape. And, R. L., don't jump to any conclusions. This isn't what it's going to sound like. I've got to go, now."

Varner crept back to the bunkroom with the telephone. Six feet from the doorway, the phonewire ran out, so he set the phone in the floor of the hallway and stretched the wire from the receiver to the phone and laid the receiver just inside the bunkroom doorway. Tonya did not move, except to press her lips together and then purse them, then press them together again. Varner returned to the office room and took the hand-sized recorder from the drawer and dropped it into the pocket of his running jacket and returned to the bunkroom. He sat in a chair at the foot of the bunk bed and removed Tonya Dawson's shoes. When he spoke, he affected a very deep, raspy voice.

"The mystery man is here."

"Who are you?"

"That would spoil everything, if you knew that."

"I don't want to spoil nothing. I don't care who you are."

"Good. That's good. The other thing is, to make this work, I have to know *everything* about you."

Varner began to massage her foot.

"Just ask. I don't have no secrets."

"The mystery man needs to know if he's got any competition. Where have you been before?"

"Everywhere."

"I need to know who."

"I got a husband."

"He any competition for the mystery man?"

"Not much. He don't last two minutes," she laughed.

"Don't laugh. The mystery man doesn't like girls who laugh. You ever do it on tape?"

"No. Not with my husband."

"You've taped him, now, haven't you, Mrs.?"

"Oh, that tape. Oh, yeah. But that's not sex."

"The mystery man doesn't care. The mystery man likes tape. He wants to know about the tape. It turns the mystery man on."

"I taped him. I just finished taping him."

Varner pressed harder against the soft sole of her foot and he slowed the motion of his hands.

"Tell the mystery man what's on the tape."

"He threatens a man."

"Who is this man?"

"Duke Taylor."

"What does he say?"

"Says if Duke doesn't pay up, he's going to take it out of his hide."

"Pay up for what?"

"The dope. Marijuana."

"Does the mystery man have any other competition? Ever been anybody else?"

"Yeah."

"Who?"

"I don't know where to start."

"What about Jack Sampson?"

"No."

"Never?"

"No. Never."

"How about girls. Do you like other girls?"

"I've done it with girls. I get hard up. I have some friends. We've gotten wrecked before and helped each other out, you know. It's okay. I like it, really."

Varner moved his hands from her foot to her calves. She groaned.

"Oh, the mystery man likes girls. Who are the girls?"

"Brenda, mostly. The girl you saw in the car with me."

"What's Brenda's last name?"

"Jarrett. It's Brenda Jarrett."

"Does Brenda have dark hair?" Varner kept his voice low.

"Yeah. You've seen her."

"You don't know who I am."

"Oh, yeah."

"Does Brenda like it, too?"

"Yeah. She's more that way than me."

"Brenda married?"

"Yeah."

"Does her husband know? Does he like it when girls do it together?"

"Lord, no. He's a redneck. If he found out, he'd die."

Varner released her legs and went to the doorway and picked up the telephone receiver and carried the phone back to the office. At the desk he whispered into the receiver.

"Did you get all that, R.L.?"

"Great. I'll bet I'll have that tape tonight. Thanks."

Varner hung up the phone and returned to the bunkroom and put Tonya Dawson's shoes back onto her feet and threw a cover across her breasts. He took the blindfold off her face.

"What are you doing? You weirdo."

"Get the tape, Tonya. You've had your screwing for tonight."

"I've had nothing. There ain't no tape."

"Oh, yeah there is, Tonya. There's at least one."

Varner pulled the recorder from his pocket and lifted the micro-cassette out of it.

"Brenda's husband will just love this one, too. Don't you think?"

"You...." She jerked against the handcuffs. They rattled against the bedposts. Her eyes were burning, her naked body twisting. "You...," she screamed.

"Just save it, Tonya. You never know, you might be being taped."

"Give me that tape."

"Trade ya."

SHE INSISTED that he carry the cassette he had shown her with him as he accompanied her to the red car, which was parked in a field of high weeds across the road from the barracks. Varner kept his gun in his other hand, hidden beneath his jacket, as they went out the front door and out of the circle of light from the barracks and across the road. She unlocked and opened the driver's-side door, and as it swung it pushed down the weeds in its arc. The dome light shone against the standing weeds, lighting the first line of them and rendering the far lines in shadow, like a thick and miniature forest. She sat in the driver's seat while Varner stood in the cleared arc. She opened a case and took out a cassette and handed it up to Varner. She had not spoken since they started for the car and now looked away, through the windshield and into the darkness, as she held her open hand up to him.

"Gimme that one," she said.

"Not yet. I've got to hear this. Put it in. Play it now."

She continued to look away from Varner and with her outstretched left hand motioned for him to return the cassette to her.

"Get in," she said.

Varner stepped back and into the weeds as she jerked the car door shut.

17

The next morning he called Maddux and told him that he had the tape but that he had listened to it only once.

"It sounded good," he said. "Dawson was raging. There is a drug case on that tape, I'm sure, and I think there may be more. Dawson threatened the guy. He said something like, 'I've hurt people before when they didn't pay me.' If that's there, we're on our way. But, my recorder's busted. I've got to get a new one or find some batteries or something."

Maddux brought batteries to the barracks and the two men listened to the tape in the little hand-held dictating machine, which was the best Varner could muster. Maddux said that they would be able to hear more of that conversation between Sam Dawson and a man Dawson called "Taylor" with a better machine, and that they would do far better if they had some headphones. Varner agreed and Maddux volunteered to go into the Bandy police station to get a better machine and a couple of headsets. Varner was exultant. He gave Maddux a key to the barracks and when Maddux left he suited up and ran his regular course around Bandy. He felt like he was gliding.

When Varner started up the hill back to the barracks at the end of his run and the barracks came in to view, he saw Maddux's cruiser rammed into the side of the quonset hut. The front end riding up on the arc of the wall, front wheels nearly off the ground, the back wheels spinning ruts in the cinders. He ran to the driver's side window, which was shattered, and saw Maddux slumped over the bloody steering wheel.

The Bandy police department building was built in 1926, when the mines were booming and the county was full of not only miners and their families, but of the butchers, bakers and candlestick makers that the miners needed to live. The red brick facade of the building was now very dirty and there was really no place from which to view it, surrounded as it was by other dirty brick buildings from the same era. But the brickwork itself was precise and ornate, the mark of an Italian stonemason whose family had immigrated to the United States and to the coalfields after World War I. Blurred by decades of soot, the arches and relief work, the complex mosaics at the top corners and top edges of the building, the soldiers—lines of brick mortared into place upright, as if standing at attention—and the sailors—lines of brick laid ends-out beneath the windows—these signatures of the fine craftsman were now virtually invisible and certainly unnoticed.

It was just after noon when Mark Varner walked into the building. It had rained and the streets and sidewalks were still damp and the sky still grey-white. The glass door, obviously not the door for which the door-frame was originally designed, pushed open and he walked in, his footsteps echoing in the hall. There were doors off this hallway. The glass panes in the doors were translucent and bore lettering "City Clerk," "Fire Chief," and "Chief of Police." Neither sound nor light came from behind any of the doors.

Varner did not go in any of these doors, but went to the end of the hallway and up the stairway and down another hallway. The wooden floorboards were worn soft and creaked with his steps. He opened a door on his right. It was marked "Booking" and opened into a large central room off of which there were several very small rooms. There were two rows of desks in the center room and no one there except Jack Sampson, who was in the small room at the very opposite of the door where Varner now stood. It was very quiet.

Sampson was seated at a desk on which there was a bottle of cola, a half-eaten sandwich, and an open newspaper. Sampson looked up at Varner as the door opened, then he looked back into the newspaper. Varner walked through the central room and stood in the doorway of the small room, across the desk from Sampson. Sampson still did not look up from the newspaper.

"We need to talk," said Varner.

"You mean *you* want something. *We* don't need anything. I don't need to talk to you."

"You want to find who killed Maddux?"

"I know who's responsible for him getting killed. You are."

"I didn't intend it, but it's true that he was where he was because of me," Varner admitted. "But, somebody did intend it."

"Did you ever notice a big difference between what you intend and what you cause? The difference between what you say and what you mean? What you tell and what you know? What you cause really happens. There are consequences for everybody."

Varner waited, but Sampson still did not look up from the newspaper.

"I know," Varner said.

"No, you don't know. You have no idea of what you're doing."

Varner did not respond.

"You don't mean what you say, either," Sampson said. "You give everybody around here the party line. This is what I can tell them, this will work, I won't tell them this."

"I have to go by the rules. You know that."

"Rules are tools between policemen." Sampson glared at Varner. "You use them as you want to. You want to play by the rules? I got rules, too. I don't share with people who don't share."

"All I can do is ask."

"You've done it."

Sampson wrapped what was left of the sandwich in waxed paper and dropped it into a trash can. He took the newspaper from the desk and folded it to quarters and put it under his arm. He took the bottle of cola, stood up and, without a glance at Varner, left the little room and walked through the big central room and out the door.

Alone now, Varner stepped across to the hat rack in the little room and carefully took Sampson's blue steel, Walton-Martin revolver from a black, patent leather holster which was draped over one arm of the hat rack. Without a sound, he pulled each cartridge from the cylinder of the revolver and laid them, one by one, on the desk and then laid the gun on the desk. He took another, identical revolver from a shoulder holster under his jacket and slid the cartridges into that gun. He took Sampson's revolver from the desk and put it into the holster under his jacket, then slipped the other gun into the holster on the rack.

PART TWO

The Story of Sampson

When the green woods laugh, with the voice of joy and the dimpling stream runs laughing by,

—*Blake*

18

A few days after Jack Sampson returned from Viet Nam in 1972, R. L. Maddux came to see him.

"Jack, you and me are goin' froggin', buddy. Like old times."

"Hell, Pop. I ain't got a license. I ain't even got a gig anymore. Not that I could find anyway. Besides, it's June. Frogs has been out of season for weeks."

"Your gig is out there on the porch," Maddux said. "I kept it nice and sharp for you; and since when did you start worryin' about licenses and seasons and the like? Ain't no warden in this county gonna arrest a war hero for gigin' a few frogs. Since you been gone the frogs around here has had it way too easy, anyway. They's a frog overpopulation. You can tell it if you listen. I brought your boots, too."

Maddux pulled the pickup onto the level spot beside the swinging bridge. It was the only place near the river wide enough to park a car. The weeds that thrived all around had given way to the frequent traffic and the narrow, sandy rectangle was strewn with litter from forbidden beer drinking and love making. When he killed the engine, the chorus of the night creatures seemed to rise. The racheting rhythms of the crickets and katydids a background for the occasional belching bass solo from a half-submerged bullfrog. It was a wild mixture of screeching and pulsing, as diverse and harmonious as creation itself. Sampson opened the gate to the truck-bed, sat down on it, and began to pull the rubber hip boots over his jeans. Maddux pulled two miner's helmets from under the truck seat and flipped on the headlamp on each of them. He put one on and brought the other one around to Sampson, who was still struggling with the long boots that fit snugly over his beefy legs.

Maddux pulled five-foot sections of half-inch copper tubing from the truck bed and twisted one into another at a homemade coupling, as if putting together a jointed pool-cue. Thus assembled, and held in the middle like a native would carry a spear, the hollow handles flexed and recoiled with each step the men took to the river. The needle-sharp gigs like miniature tridents whipping up and down, flashing in and out of the long cones of light from the helmets. They would work the shallow backwater below the bridge at the mouth of Mud Creek, then head up the little stream.

The hunters entered the water as silently as landing ducks, their shadows silhouetted dimly in the backglow of the headlamps. They stepped carefully, side by side, moving upstream and toward the other bank. They were knee deep in the wide pool and nearing the opposite bank when they stopped simultaneously, without obvious cue, as if reading from the same musical score.

The beams from the headlamps, long, smokey cones, scanned the water's edge like searchlights, the tall thin man looking left, the stocky man to the right. Outside the scope of the beams, the water was black, the creek-bank black. The right-angling beam stopped abruptly and was immediately joined by the other beam. Under the doubled brightness a foot-long bullfrog squatted, motionless as a statue, blinded and nearly incapacitated by the light. He will not move until he is touched. Then, unless pierced, his powerful legs would propel him out of the narrow beam and into the wet darkness. The first stroke must kill.

The tall man, without turning his head, eyed his partner. The broad-backed man with an overhand motion drew his gig back then stabbed it into the circle of light. The sound is unmistakable: an almost human groan as the life escapes from the inflated creature. A light beam wiggled up and down as the Maddux nodded his head. He smiled as he whispered.

"I swear, Jack, you ain't lost a thing."

Sampson's teeth showed as he smiled. "It's been six years since I done that if it's been a day," he said.

The pair continued up the creekbed, away from the river. With each turn the stream grew steeper and rockier. They moved slowly enough to count each stone, constantly surveying the waterline. They passed wordlessly through layers of air, each cooler than the last, as in a cave. The creek smells were of moss, pine, sassafras, damp rotting leaves. The familiar holes all seemed to give up frogs, and the onion sack on Sampson's belt soon bulged with twitching carcasses.

Neither man was suspicious of the other's silence. Speech was unnecessary between them, familiar as they were with the stream and the technique; it would only serve to alert their quarry. Nonetheless, as they first heard the splashing of the waterfall, words rushed through their minds. The hunt would end at the waterfall. The stream above it was too small to support a good frog population; it was not worth the climb. They would pull out, as always, at the Giant's Chair, an outcrop of sandstone roughly the shape of a couch. It was ritual. There hunt would be recounted. There was the place for words.

Maddux had his speech well planned. It, not frogs, was the real purpose of this trip. Things had to be right. These were important words. He repeated them in his mind.

Sampson's thoughts were neither orderly nor assured. His mind was near bursting with a thought that had obsessed him for years. A thought he carried with him during his eighteen-month tour in southeast Asia. A thought that he had always found impossible to express. In Nam somehow the ache of it had been duller. There his hope was simple and well-defined: to return home. Somehow, if he could only go home and to the things that had surrounded her—the things that had surrounded them—the next step would come. It would just happen; he was so sure of that. But the next step did not come. Here he was, where he had so longed to be, and it was no answer at all. He seemed to be standing at the threshold of a door that would not open. Now he did not even know what to hope for. This thing, this experience, was so far removed from anything else he had known that to speak of it seemed to require a foreign language—a language he had only once spoken and, even then, had not known. He had spoken it and he had heard it in a fit of ecstasy like the tongues at Pentecost. And now those few to whom he had spoken it were gone—and the words, those strange, beautiful words, were but dim and incomprehensible echos.

Could he talk to R.L. about it? He was afraid not. In the absence of the spirit it would be just babble. How could it be said without sounding pathetic, selfish, foolish? It was howling for the moon, and R. L. would see it for that. Jack could not imagine R.L., or anyone else he knew for that matter, feeling the way he did.

What in the world could anybody say about it anyway? He just wanted something he couldn't have. It was that simple if you took a hard look at it.

Maddux was having no such struggle. His plans were made, his words were chosen.

"Jack," Maddux said as he laid aside his gig, "I want to talk to you about the union."

The girl's name was Libby Moss. She had sat in front of him in senior English class and, until a day in April, he had never noticed her. There was, to put it lightly, a very fixed social order at Sherman High School in 1969. The girls there understood the concept of a union and, unless you were a dues-paying member, you never got a shot at a football player. Not that it had ever mattered to Jack Sampson. Things were working like they ought to as far as he had been concerned. He never missed a party, and the interludes between girlfriends were so short as to hardly be noticeable. Bliss is ignorance.

"Jack," Maddux continued, "the union needs new leaders. I've had the responsibility at 2094 now for twenty-five years—since I got back from the war."

Although Libby Moss was aware of the enforced stratification within the school, she paid the cliques no attention and no tribute. A mature person would have seen this as maturity. In the main, the girls considered it a snub—and a threat. After all, the boys are just boys. Unsophisticated and easily fooled. It is the girls who know which girls are really beautiful.

"That's one thing that made me ready to be a leader here, Jack. I had to march under far. I had to believe in the righteousness of my cause enough to risk my life over it. This war—between the company and the workin' man—it don't ever end and somebody has to keep the troops marchin'. You know what I'm sayin', Jack ?"

And Libby Moss was beautiful. Tall with high cheek-bones and a glorious mane of hair that carried the shades of autumn and the radiance of spring, hers was the beauty of the chestnut filly.

"I do, R.L., I think I do," Sampson answered. He was sitting back in the Giant's Chair, staring into the river of stars overhead. *The diamond sky.* He began to double down the hip-boots. *To dance beneath the diamond sky with one hand waving free...*

Although her beauty remained unnoticed, it was not because of any deliberate attempt to mask it. It was because of differing definitions of beauty. Libby Moss had come to Boone County from Columbus, Ohio at the beginning of the school year. Her father, David, was a sociology professor at Case Western Reserve University. He had accepted a tour of duty at a community college in the next county in the hope of advancing his research on his doctoral dissertation on the United Mineworkers of America. He was a favorite personality within the university community, in part because of his whole-hearted devotion to his subject and in part for his brilliance as a classical pianist.

The things that were accepted as worthy by the Boone County crowd were not so impressive to Libby Moss. "She lives in her own damn little world," the girls said of her. It was one way to look at it. Another was that she simply was not attracted to life in their own damn little world.

"I want you to run for Local President this time, Jack." Not a muscle in Maddux' face moved. "I want you to take my place."

It was hard to answer him. Maddux was asking for blood, he knew he was asking for blood. Still, he was the kind who would not ask unless someone else was dying.

"I don't know, R.L. I don't think I want to get involved in all of that right now. I don't even know how long I'm gonna stay in the coal mines."

"You are already involved in it, Jack. You're involved in it every time you go underground. You can ignore it. Lord knows, that's the problem with these new guys—things are fairly good right now, oil prices is up and everbody's buyin' coal. Wages are decent, too— thanks to the battles the union fought over the last twenty years. These guys don't understand that. Things are pretty good now—work is plentiful and steady and wages are pretty good. That's all they see. There ain't a one of 'em I know that could step in and do the job."

Libby Moss had sat right in front of him in senior English class. Mrs. Pauley had assigned the class—each member of the class—to write a poem.

"This time in your lives," she had told her class, "is a very special time. It is a time you will always remember. I want you to write a poem about your feelings—how you feel about graduation—how you feel about leaving school—how you see your experiences in high school

now that you look back on them. I want you to take some time on this one. Do your best work. This should be something you will want to save and look back on."

It had been a bleak winter. Since his father's death in the explosion at Catton Number Two, Jack Sampson had opted out of the whirl of dates and parties that had been normal for him. At first it had been impossible to sleep. He had begun a diary. That was some comfort— to write it down. Those things he could share with absolutely no one—the despair, the hurt, the fear, and— most of all—the guilt. These things flowed into the diary page by page, hour by hour, and night by night. He took walks—slipping out of the house after midnight—down to the river. The Walhonde River, which as long as Jack Sampson could remember had run black as a storm cloud. That winter, Jack would often leave his room through his bedroom window and walk zombie-like to the riverbank. There he would stare till dawn into the sooty, grey ice.

It was in a basketball game in gym class that he first noticed how his physical strength had waned. He was out in front on a fast-break and the lead pass to him was perfect. He took the pass and, as he approached the basket, tried to stop to make the leap to the basket. But he could not stop himself. His legs would not accept the stress. They buckled and Sampson slammed into the gymnasium wall beneath the basket.

Pride is a powerful thing, and it was pride that got him started on a weightlifting program. In the gym by himself for two or three hours after school each day, he worked to regain and surpass his former strength. The discipline, the measurable progress toward a goal, and the catharsis of physical exhaustion made sleep possible again. This was his therapy and the renewed soundness of body was peace. He wrote a final entry in his diary. It was a poem. A poem about hope restored, about the joy of existence, about being satisfied with life as it is. It was the only poem in the diary and a fitting way to close it. This was what Jack Sampson brought to English class in response to Mrs. Pauley's assignment.

"We are going to read some of the poems aloud today," Mrs. Pauley said. "You do not have to read your own. You may pass your composition to someone else to read if you wish."

"Here," he whispered to Libby Moss, "I don't want to read this thing. I didn't know she was gonna make us do this. You read this, okay?"

Libby Moss was the best creative writer in the class and was not intimidated by reading her work. Mrs. Pauley called on her first to get things started. She stood up to read Jack's poem:

"This is in two parts," she said. "The first part is a little different from the second, but it's the same voice throughout. The second part is kind of a response to the first."

She focused on the page.

I said to the mountain "Let me go. I have a
life to live."
I said to the mountain, but he said "No, for
I have life to give."
I said to the mountain "You are a thief. You
just take life away."
"But," said the mountain "you can't see. Wait
for another day."
   The reader paused here, looked into the hostile little
audience, then continued,

Something wakes me without sounding
Nothing stirs, I hear my breath
I look out my bedroom window
Into darkness, into death.

Yet I move the blanket over
Shiver with the morning cold
I look through my tiny window
Still the darkness, all is old.

And yet I heed the voice that calls me
Down the stairs and there I see
My father's full and tended table
And there a plate and cup for me.

Fed and clothed, I start my journey
With a strength that conquers night
I walk through an open doorway
Into morning, into light.

A boy sitting on the front row had been saving a large fart for the ending. He let it go masterfully, a patented two-noter, just as Libby Moss had reverently sounded the last syllable. Everyone laughed.

After class, Libby Moss caught Jack, who was in a hurry to escape.

"That was a beautiful poem," she said. "It shouldn't bother you that they acted like they did. They thought it was mine. They didn't really hear the poem. They just don't like me. But it is a beautiful poem. I love it. I'm going to keep a copy. I know just what you were saying. I have felt the same way about this place—at least the way that is in the first part. I feel so alone here sometimes. I'm surprised you wrote this. I would never have guessed that you felt those things."

"Thanks. I thought it was good. I thought you did a good job reading it." Sampson could not suppress a smile. "You understood it right off the bat. It surprises me some of the things I feel these days. I keep thinking something is going to happen. Something big and good is going to happen."

Libby Moss looked around the emptying hall, she crossed her arms, holding her elbows in her hands, tilted her head, then spoke very quickly. "Come to the choral program tonight. You'll love it. There's a song in the program I want you to hear." Then Libby Moss, who sat in front of Jack Sampson in senior English class, and who was looking better all the time, vanished into a classroom.

That afternoon the windows were open in the school weight room and the flat, steamy, sweaty smells were gone. It almost seemed like another room, even another building; the sunlight and the breeze laden with the clean scent of thawing earth had taken away the dinginess. It was the same concrete floor and unpainted cinderblock walls, but today Jack saw a kind of spartan beauty in the simple order. It was pure. Its shape was determined by its function. It was a place for work and there was no frill to detract from the theme. He felt himself its master.

His solitary workout was almost noiseless: the occasional clunk of plate against bar, the muted push of the barbell lowered into the mat. He watched the black iron move up and down, in and out. It was effortless— as if the massive objects were self-propelled or moved in response to a force outside his body.

This world is full of wasted potential: of lawyers who should have been mechanics and salesmen who should have sung opera. But Jack Sampson in a weight room was a picture of a shoe that fit and today, more than ever, he felt himself in bloom. Today he did not work himself to exhaustion; he worked through the first sweat and until he felt his arms and legs tight as steel bands. Exhaustion now took hours and curtain time for the choral program was seven-thirty. Besides, tonight he did not want to be exhausted. Tonight he wanted to see and hear everything. Something good was going to happen—something big and good. Somehow the old pattern of things had been broken. He could feel it, and as he left the locker room he shivered with excitement. He could feel it in his immortal and fearsome frame.

Jack felt a little self-conscious as he entered the school auditorium. In his three years at the school, he had been in this room only once: to take a college entrance test. There were a few others seated: Mrs. Pauley, of course, a few other teachers, some with their husbands, and a sparse scattering of people he did not recognize Jack was surprised that almost no one in the crowd gave any indication that they recognized him. He read the program from the page an usher had handed him on the way in. "The Sherman Chorus presents The Sound of Music ". He looked away at a young mother seated with two small children near the front of the room. The little boy was looking at the high ceiling and pointing here and there as if at a fancied bird or airplane. Everyone in the place is dressed up, Jack thought as he returned his attention to the printed page:

The Sherman High School Chorus
presents selections from
The Rogers and Hammerstein musical
"The Sound of Music"

Director: Mr. Charles Kimble
Accompanist: Mr. David Moss
The chorus, Mr. Kimble, and Sherman High
all wish to express their sincere appreciation
to Mr. David Moss for his immeasurable con-
tribution in the preparation for and perform-
ance of this program. We are indeed fortunate
to have him with us in this undertaking.

I didn't know she had a brother. This David Moss
must be her brother, Jack thought. A bearded man in a
charcoal suit walked out from behind the curtain, stage
right. He sat down at the black baby grand piano and,
hands on thighs, studied a few sheets of music arranged
on the piano. Then he lowered his face and closed his
eyes, as if he were in prayer. All shuffling and whisper-
ing in the little audience stopped.

He began with a one-hand chord. It was a serious
sound, ending with just a layer of brightness. Around the
resonance, the other hand began to weave a pattern of
notes, each measured and understated. At once the music
was deeply familiar and completely strange to Jack. It
was the near familiarity of a half-remembered dream; a
lullaby from another life. The piece lifted from one tem-
pered and controlled chord to another, the melody glid-
ing like a skater over the smooth and flawless surface of
tones. Jack found himself anticipating, and half hoping
for a resolution of the enchanting vibrations which

seemed almost tangible now, not originating within the instrument, but suspended and radiating from an invisible center somewhere above the piano. He was hoping unconsciously for a return to tonic chord, to the fully stated note, to some familiar change. Half hoping for some return, some statement of the familiar and half hoping to be carried away to an unknown and glorious world—a bright and inexpressible place he had surely once known but till now forgotten.

At first, Jack did not recognize Libby Moss. The chorus stood on a three-tiered bandstand, center stage. She was on the middle level at the end of the row, he thought. That must be her. None of the others could be. But he wasn't sure. This girl—this woman—seemed taller, and strands of her hair were drawn back loosely and fell in layers on her shoulders like the fine feathers of a dove. Tall, flawless, and so well-defined, bold here, subtle there, nothing shrinking or apologetic. The beauty of a new tulip. Maybe it wasn't her. Maybe she for some reason had not come tonight. It was a smile that gave her away. It was a badge of sincerity, and a thousand words of welcome and delight. It was her smile; still, it was not familiar. He was thirty feet away, just thirty feet away, and it took him seemingly forever to see the obvious: this woman—this graceful creature dressed in a royal gown—was Libby Moss who had sat in front of him in senior English class all year and he did not know her at all.

One thing he did recognize immediately was the song he was there for, the one he had been invited to hear. It was "Climb Every Mountain." That had to be it. It was her solo and after she sang it Jack walked out of the auditorium. He had to do this because people didn't really know him. People did not really understand everything there was to understand about him, and they would have mistaken it. People were always mistaking the deep things, they always did. People would not have understood the tears that he was unable to suppress. The tears he had himself been unconscious of until he felt them streaking down his cheeks. People would have taken that for something pitiful or pathetic. "Something must've reminded him of his dad," they would say. And they would be wrong. "His dad must've sung that song," they would say. And they would be wrong. He was reminded of his father, but not in the way they thought. This feeling that was not from the words but from the music was a feeling he had first felt with the passing of his father. Death, in bringing life to an end, somehow had allowed him a glimpse of it as a whole. The overwhelming sweetness and the heartbreaking beauty of this moment of life we are given. People would not understand this; there would be no explaining it to them, and so he left the auditorium at the end of the song.

How was he to approach her? The show was over, but they had made no plan. He would go backstage—that was at least polite—she would expect that. But what would he say? What do you say when the world has moved under your feet? How do you work that into a conversation with a stranger? The little audience had dispersed and the hallways of the school were empty. On his way to the music room, Jack's footfalls echoed. The school felt different at night—uncrowded and unrushed. All light was from the overhead fixtures and the hallway somehow looked to Jack more adult, less like a school. Jack for a moment imagined he was in some kind of airbase in England. He was a pilot and his flight—a spy mission over Germany—would leave at midnight. He walked to the work entrance of the backstage area.

"Jack, you're smarter than I thought you were. Libby Moss, huh?" Charlie Callihan was leaving the music room. Charlie was the punter for the football team. He had been a classmate of Jack's for twelve years and this greeting was the most he had ever heard Charlie utter at one time. Hmm, that feels good. He knows—she must be telling people. Even with that he might have stumbled, he might have been effusive and too intense for a first date, but for the fact that this medieval princess, this nightingale, was playing a game of hoops as he approached the music room. A game with a ball of crumpled notebook paper. The goal was a green steel wastebasket. This was his kind of opening. Unseen, he reached through the doorway and caught a long jumpshot just before it dropped into the goal.

"Jack."

It was the first time he had heard Libby say his name.

He stepped into the room, pivoted and sunk an unlikely bank shot off the front of the teacher's desk.

There were four of them: Jack and Libby and Charlie and Stephanie Lantz. Stephanie had sung alto with Libby and Charlie had been somewhere in the auditorium.

"Can you come over for a while?" Libby asked. "Mom and Dad have fixed a bunch of food for the chorus."

"I'm starving," said Jack, who had not noticed it till then. "Mom is over at her sister's in Columbus. I haven't even gone home yet."

Even though the Moss's home was spacious, it was not really big enough for the chorus and their entourage of parents, teachers, girlfriends and boyfriends. Jack found himself on a patio, content for the moment with a plate heaped with party meatballs, fancy crackers and cheese. He was talking to Charlie Callihan.

"Do you know any of these people?" Jack asked Charlie.

"I know who some of them are." He snickered. "I know who Stephanie is…I know who Libby Moss is. But I don't know any of them very well. Including Stephanie."

"Buddy, I don't know anybody either…I don't know what to do. I don't know if I'm supposed to leave with the rest of these people or stick around. I don't even know where Libby is."

"Stick around, Jack. Libby will be around when things thin down. The word I get is that Libby likes you. You want to stick around for that, don't you?"

"Oh, yeah...oh, yeah."

The record player was in the basement. It was a kind of den or family room—carpeted, with a couch, a couple of chairs, and a woodstove. But the center of it all, as far as Libby was concerned, was the stereo.

"What kind of music do you like?" she asked.

"I don't know. I like about all music. I like to dance."

Libby was on her knees, flipping through a horizontal column of record albums. "How about Dylan? You like Dylan?"

"Dillon who?" Jack asked. "Is it like that stuff your dad played tonight on the piano? I liked that."

Libby Moss smiled. "No, it's not like that at all. But you've got to hear him. Not everyone likes him, but I love him." She pulled a dark colored album from the column, took the record from the sleeve and dropped it onto the turntable. "Listen. This may take awhile."

It took awhile. About eight hours to be precise. Time and again Jack wondered when the door at the top of the stairs would open and an adult voice, polite, but with a hint of outrage, would say, 'Do you all know what time it is?' He finally asked her.

"Your parents are bound to be going crazy. It's two in the morning. We've got school in the morning."

"Don't worry about it. They don't mind. I'm down here to all hours all the time anyway. I get wrapped up in this music."

That was some reassurance, but Jack's thought had been that they might have been concerned about something other than the lateness of the hour. No matter, he thought. The other thing they might have been worrying about was not happening anyway. There had been no suggestion that it was going to happen either. This was strange to a young man whose long meetings with young women usually shared characteristics with a big-time wrestling match: there was always some element of feigned physical resistance, someone was always keeping score, and, no matter how impassioned it might have looked, it was all for show.

But things were happening. He did not know this girl and he did not know this music, but he liked them both. This music was full of riddles, things were not so much said as mentioned in passing. Things were said about one thing, not to be about that thing, but to suggest to you something else. There was all this talk of freedom, talk of dancing and a sky of diamonds. There was with it a sensation of flight. There was a vision of the limitless, appeals to the unconscious. Where had he been? There was so much here to appreciate. How could he have failed to see it? Sitting right in front of him for seven months. Here was mystery—something subtle. Something to be learned. Something to explore. Words came slowly at first—what if he sounded stupid? But that fear was quickly overcome. One thing the girl could do was listen. She seemed to be entertained with all his ramblings, asking questions—sometimes deep, sometimes silly. If you hit the ball somewhere in baseball and someone catches it, why is that not a hit? What do you think about the end of the world? *All of the time she sat in the floor—sometimes arms wrapped around her bent legs, her chin resting on her knees. God, she was easy to look at.*

The end of the world. He had thought about it. There was a lot of stuff in the Bible about that: soldiers neck deep in blood, stars falling from the sky. It was a terrible thing. He didn't think about it much. He didn't like to think about it.

"It's apocalyptic," she said. "That stuff about the stars and all—that's a kind of writing. My dad says those things are symbols—they don't mean that the thing described is actually going to happen. They mean the end of the world—not the physical destruction of the planet—but the ending of an old order."

"This is wild. Why do you think about stuff like this?"

"My dad, mainly—and Bob Dylan. My dad is a Bible teacher—he's a lot of things really..."

"He sure can play the piano."

"He's a very smart man. He's good at a lot of things. Anyway, he is always trying to get me interested in the Bible. One day I was down here listening to Dylan, and

Dad was in the shop—right in there—I didn't even know he was in there. Anyway, I'm listening to Dylan— I've got the thing cranked way up—a song ends and Dad sticks his head through the doorway. It scared me out of my wits. He said 'That's apocalyptic…'"

"What…what's apocalyptic?"

"It was a song that used all kinds of crazy images and talked about the end of the present order."

"So?"

"Well, that's not all he said, of course. He went on talking about the Book of Revelation and telling me what 'apocalyptic' means."

"So, what's it mean?"

"If it's real, true stuff—if it's really inspired—people see signs—they see signs that mean something—the ending of an age, an order, a power. They take this inspiration and convert it into symbols that other people can understand. But not just anybody can understand them. You have to be tuned in. You have to be sensitive to them."

"That's pretty heavy. I still don't understand why you're so fascinated by it."

"I think the world is ending." She smiled as she said it. "I do. I think things are changing fast. I think people are changing. Like you. You wouldn't have written that poem at the beginning of the year. There are other things, too. This music is so strong. I think there is a new world coming."

"What other things?"

"The anti-war movement," for example.

It was only after the conversation had stopped for a while that Jack again thought about time. There was sunlight coming through a window. He filled with doubt and uncertainty as he rose to leave. What do I say? What does she expect? What has happened here tonight? He was sure he did not want to leave it here, whatever it was. Whatever it was, he wanted to keep it going. What could he say or do to get that across? How did one express the sublime.

"I've got to get going." It was all he could manage— too much would be worse than too little, he sensed. This was one girl that didn't need—didn't want—things to be mapped out. "I've got to change these clothes before school starts." That sounded right—like he did this kind of thing all the time. Sat up all night alone with a beautiful girl and talked about the world coming to an end—he did this all the time.

Then there was another smile. It was as if he had somehow found the magic spell. She smiled—it was a smile that told him this is what I had suspected about you—what I had hoped for. It was a smile that said, in a sort of apocalyptic way: I've had a great time tonight, let's do it again very soon.

That was the smile she smiled as she stood up and walked him to the basement door. It was the smile she smiled again as she kissed him and the world ended.

Six in the morning, the first day of May. The sun was at his back as he began the walk home. There were no sounds, no cars, no birds, no breeze. The thing people didn't understand about apocalypse, one of the things anyway, was that the old—the thing that died—was replaced by the new—something better. The forested hills stretched their arms in the new light, the dogwood and redbud blossoming beneath the still naked hardwoods: a white and pink undergarment, subtle and fine. The sun on his back began to warm him, relaxing his muscles. It was a toasty warmth—like a blanket. He closed his eyes, then again. There, just ahead, was a dry place, covered with last year's leaves. Sampson lay down.

Then he was in another place. Alone, he stood at the edge of a wheat field. He was surrounded by the pleas-ant dryness and vibrant colors of indian summer. The grain was golden and ripe—brittle enough to whisper as a soft wind blew over it. He could not see the end of the field in any direction, although he did not look back. This was not home—the field went on flat to the horizon. He did not move, but in the moment that he was there he sensed two things. One was the aroma the breeze lifted off of the field. It was a mixture of cut grass, baking bread and something else, something he could not place. With it, perhaps because of it, came a feeling—he had not really ever felt it before—it was a little like the way he had felt the evening he had com-pleted the roof on his uncle's barn. That had been a daunting task for a fifteen year old and one that had required him to pull off a day's worth of mistakes and start all over again. But he had finished it. Late in the afternoon he had come down the ladder and stood away in the pasture, looking at the perfect, finished roof. This feeling was a little like that. But it was more. There was something in this feeling about the unseen end of the wheatfield. There was something in it that said: you can walk here, there is much to be seen ahead, and it is wonderful. It is all new, and you can go there alone. Not "you must go there alone", but "you may." The other part of the sensation was the utter satisfaction he felt in the complete solitude. He was free, complete, and nothing lay ahead of him but promise.

When he awoke, he was at first confused and a bit troubled—not only at the vividness of the dream and at his own uncertainty of its meaning, but because he had been alone in the dream. He was troubled that the dream, following so close on the heels of his evening with Libby Moss, seemed to have nothing to do with her. There was no Libby Moss in the dream and there was no music. There was no sensation of flight. The most vivid and unexplained effect of the dream was to leave him with a throbbing awareness of his physical strength that he had never before known. Last summer he had carried mortar for a crew of bricklayers. After he had struggled the first few days with the shovel and wheelbarrow handles, all coarse and sharp with dried splashes of mortar, a worker had offered him a pair of leather work gloves. Then what had been agony seemed easy. The gloves, in protecting him from the rough edges of the job, seemed to give his hands added strength. Now, as he walked, he felt that same sense of protection and power. It was as if his whole body was protected by a tight leather glove. All of this with a quiet and sober sense of peace. But even with that, there was a piece of it missing. That which he remembered hinted at that which he had forgotten—that which had quickly tumbled back into subconscious. It seemed that maybe the biggest part of it was already gone—perhaps the part that would allow him some understanding. He sat down in the leaves and closed his eyes, reviewing as closely as possible that which he remembered. But the dream was recorded on thin film and when stopped too long in one place the image began to curl and fade in the bright light of consciousness. There was a risk of losing it all. Maybe it would come back another time. Jack brushed bits of leaves from his jeans and restarted his walk home.

As he began walking, he felt himself in the dream. Yes, that was it—there was a cadence to the dream—a pace—somewhere between a heartbeat and a march. It was the pace of a walk, a deliberate walk. He slowed his stride to match the sensed meter. Now it will come back, he thought.

And maybe it would have, had Jack been able to keep the rhythm—if he had not heard the shrieks of the little girl—if he had not seen the five Doberman pinschers tearing down the mountainside, knocking the tiny child to her back.

Jack was thirty yards away and nearing the crest of a hill when he saw the attack. He ran straight to the child at open field speed. As he approached, one of the five dogs ran toward Sampson. The animal was glossy black and had its teeth bared in a madman's grin. Tense and shivering with its predatory purpose, it leapt at Sampson's face. Sampson, without breaking stride, cocked his fist behind him like an outfielder ready to peg a ball home. Once the dog was airborne, it was powerless to slip the punch that came with all the force that the nineteen year old all-state fullback could muster: calves, thighs, hips, chest and arms—every fiber of muscle whipped the fist forward. Sampson hit the flying Doberman under its jaw, twisting its neck to Sampson's left and whirling its entire body a half-turn, the dog's legs flailing as it dropped to the ground. It circled to its right, bug-eyed, following its now misaligned snout and pulling wildly at its contorted neck. Another dog had grabbed Sampson by his left leg, another had run away, two were still locked onto the screaming child. Sampson walked to the child, seemingly oblivious to the growling Doberman ripping into his jeans. He waved his arms and screamed at the top of his lungs.

The dogs were like swine at a feeding trough, they did not even look up. Sampson knelt to the ground and reached around each dog's neck, grabbing each dog under the jaw. He slid his fingers down the taut skin until he found the bony throat. The dogs made gagging sounds and pushed away with their rear legs, trying to escape the suffocating grasp as Sampson closed each hand, snapping the canines' windpipes as easily as one might crack one's knuckles. The remaining dog released Sampson's leg and fled.

The child's mother ran from her small home. She was wearing a pink housecoat, holding it together at breast level with one hand. She fell hysterically beside her rescued daughter, overcome with terror and relief.

But there is more: she was a religious woman, the wife of a pastor, and a student of the Scriptures. And she had just seen a sign.

LIBBY MOSS was certain that her destiny did not lay in Boone County. It was quite possible, even probable, she thought, that the fate of Jack Sampson did. It would be unfair then not to let him know that. But no, that was too much to say. It sounded condescending. The thing to do, the fair thing to do, was to not let things go too far. Just don't mislead the guy, that would be easy enough. There were only six weeks of school

*left and she had led a nun's life her whole year here any-
way; she was practiced at being aloof.*

*But the world was ending. That was the complica-
tion. Now, as of the last week, as of the night with Jack
and the newspaper article about the pastor's daughter,
everyone was her friend. And Jack, what a guy. She
felt—she knew—that she had already gotten to him and
it was a feeling of delight and responsibility.*

*Who really knew, anyway? Who could really say
what would happen tomorrow? She would not just end
the thing. There was something to it. Maybe she didn't
know as much as she had thought. She would let things
take their course. Live life—take each day as it came.*

*And oh, the days did come. Each spring is just a little
different than all the others. There is a different balance
between the sunny and rainy days, a different mixture
of wildflower smells in the air, a different set of songs
on the radio. Spring is the magic season, but each
spring has a magic all its own. In the spring of 1969,
with six weeks to go in the school year and less than
eight months left in the decade, the sixties came to
Boone County. It was like an explosion. It was a thing
that had been waiting to happen. An old order had lost
its grip. It had been ready to die. There were splashes of
vivid color in the classrooms. The buttoned-down was
now the tie-dyed. Most of all, there was new music:
enchanting, beckoning, exciting. Music of a new world.*

Then there was the river. For eleven million years that stream that the Indians had named Walhonde had run out of the Appalachian Mountains. In that time it had churned and polished away ton upon ton of its sandstone cradle till it at last ran in a smooth, sandy channel. The river flowed generally west-south-west and, on late summer afternoons, the crystalline, wide, shallow stretches made magnificent ballrooms for the long-angled sunlight.

In those days—in that short, sweet season—Jack Sampson stood in the favor of the rare maiden.

The town of Bandy was settled along the banks of the Walhonde in 1912, when the Red Parrot Coal Company opened the first deep mine in the county. By 1923, the company had erected a steel suspension bridge across the stream to allow workers from the other side access to the mine. The bridge was designed for foot traffic only.

The swinging bridge, as it was called, was only a couple of feet above water and the band of shadow it cast across the river did not vary much during the day. The banks beneath the bridge stayed mossy. In the hottest part of summer, the long steel cables which arced down from the posts would expand with dull, clanking sounds, as if someone had hit them with a sledge.

Before the wash plant, boys from town would lie prone across the bridge and dangle looped banjo strings into the water. Red-tailed suckers and channel catfish would lay just a few inches below the surface, facing upstream, motionless as rocks in the slow current. When a wire noose surrounded one of the lethargic fish, the youngster would snap the loop closed, jerking the quarry, flopping and shivering, onto the wooden planks.

The wash-plant changed all that. Since its installation in 1961, the river had run black and carried the tarry, sulfurous smells of the coal-mines.

In the spring of 1969, the spring of Jack Sampson and Libby Moss, the United Mine Workers of America began a strike which would last almost nine months and would change permanently the economy and the demographics of Boone County. During that strike the wash-plants closed. The river was clear the next day. The golden sandy bottom reappeared, now tiger-striped with streaks of coal dust.

With an instinct as sure and as nautical as that of spawning salmon, the high school kids quickly found the old swimming holes and flocked to them. There were trucks and motorbikes parked in bunches on the riverbanks. Honor Society girls snuck out of bedroom windows in t-shirts and jeans. They learned something old, something long-lost: there was medicine in the river water. The Indians had known that. Sunny afternoons turned into cool evenings and the children of the new order sat sun-dried around campfires, relaxed and changed.

Above it all hovered the tamborine man, invisible to all, audible only to those with ears to hear. He was with them in their cars, in their bedrooms, and on the river-bank. Everyday he sang a new song. The old things had passed away.

It was spring, it was 1969, and Jack Sampson was in love. Things that had sounded with a dull thud now began to jingle-jangle.

IT SEEMED that the leader of the change was Jack Sampson. He was, after all, a leader. He saved the little girl, and he refused to bean Tim Lintz with a dodgeball.

The name of the game was warball. The gym teacher would have the whole class line up along the out-of-bounds line and count off one-two, one-two: the ones on one side of the gym, the twos on the other. Seven or eight dodgeballs would be laid out along the half-court line. Then a mad rush for the balls and a throwing frenzy. For the first few minutes of the match the sounds of the balls slapping flesh and the echos resounding in the gym took on the relentless rhythm of a boxer's speed bag. If you caught a ball, the thrower was out and rele-gated to the bleachers. If a ball hit you and you did not catch it, you were out and on the bleachers. The bad thing was getting blindsided. There were always more balls in play than you could keep track of, particularly in the early going. An unanticipated dodgeball to the temple could result, and had resulted, in a ruptured eardrum or concussion. It was a simple, brutal game that required no planning, thought, or supervision. In fact, once the game was underway, the coaches often ducked into the coaches' lounge for a cigarette.

And the kids loved it. As the bleachers grew more and more crowded with eliminated players, the din in the gymnasium would reach deafening levels. The contest between the last few survivors usually took on the flavor of a battle between gladiators. In the next to last game of warball to be played at Sherman High School, Jack Sampson was the apparent winner. There was nothing apocalyptic about that. Jack Sampson was normally the winner in warball. But in this game he was only the apparent winner. The bleachers on Sampson's side of the gym had gone wild as Sampson eliminated Jim Terry, the last apparent two on the floor. But as the cheers subsided, Coach Clark walked onto the floor, handed Sampson a ball, and pointed toward a section of bleachers behind which hid Tim Lintz, all 105 pounds of him. The coach yelled at Lintz to come out. He crawled out from underneath a low bleacher, red-faced and shaking. Both sides of the gym raised catcalls at the doomed freshman.

Sampson, in a reflex, took the ball and began walking toward Lintz. The bloodthirsty crowd was roaring.

Then Sampson stopped. He laid the ball down and the gym fell silent.

Coach Clark was not amused. He banished Sampson to the showers and yelled at him for all to hear, "That'll cost you a letter grade, Sampson." But it was too late: the lion had lain down with the lamb.

Coach Clark laid the balls out at half-court again and blew his whistle: the signal for the beginning of the melee. There was no mad dash for the balls from either side and no effort to slam one another with them. The students walked to the half-court line and once there just picked the balls up and began tossing them to each other as if they were on a picnic. Clark was without an ally. He acknowledged defeat by sending the whole class to the showers.

It was a new day.

While it seemed like Jack Sampson was the beginning of the revolution at Sherman High, Jack himself was one of the few who knew this to be false—who knew that Libby Moss was the true prophet of the apocalypse. Jack was one of those few and Charlie Callihan was another. Since the night with Libby, Jack had begun to share everything with Charlie, particularly those things about Libby.

CHARLIE PLAYED left field for Sherman High and on right-handed hitters, played close enough to the foul line to hear Jack Sampson as he yelled from his motorbike just outside the fence, "Let's get out of here, Charlie."

Callihan unbent out of his fielder's crouch and looked over at Sampson. "Four more innings."

"Four more innings nothin'. It's gonna rain, man. No way you'll ever finish this game. Let's get out of here now. I want to get to the river before it starts rainin'. I want to go swimmin'."

"Hey, what am I gonna do, Jack? There are four more innings. I've been killing this pitcher."

"I gotta talk to ya, man."

The last phrase was from the new language. Its meaning could only be known within the brotherhood. That brotherhood which had in the last three weeks learned something about the urgency of time, which knew that there were some things, some very valuable things, which had to be said now—while they were felt. Otherwise these things, these things that were happening so fast, would vanish with only the most unsatisfying trace left behind. Charlie had known it to happen. Something so profound, so urgent, had pressed against him and then, unexpressed, it was gone. He could remember that it had come, when it had come, and a bit of what it had felt like, but he could not remember the thing itself. These things had to be said or they were lost.

That is why Charlie Callihan made no effort to explain to anyone as he, glove in hand, jumped the left-field fence, *boarded the back of Jack Sampson's motorbike, and sped away with one out in the fifth.*

There was a time and a place for such things. The time was always now and the place was always the riverbank. It was raining now, a cold spring rain. Charlie's uniform was drenched and he shivered and chilled as the bike raced along the narrow river road. As Sampson killed the engine a sharp crack of thunder shook the ground.

"That's close. It doesn't sound that way unless it's close," said Charlie.

"That's good. There's nothin' like a little lightning to liven up a swim." Jack was shucking his shirt.

"You aren't going in there in this are you, man?" Charlie was shaking as he spoke, rain dripping from the bill of his baseball cap.

"Why not? It'll clean out your sinuses."

Charlie looked across the river at the tall sycamore that angled over the stream. He knew the knot of roots at its base was usually above the water. Now it was sub-merged, covered over by the swollen current that ran rust-red. The river was dull and opaque and would have seemed almost solid but for the billions of frigid rain-drops that pelted its surface, each smacking with a white splash and a sound that, taken all together, seethed and pulsed like a waterfall. Tiny black rafts of twigs, leaves, and dead grass swirled in the middle of the channel marking the river's rise and accelerated flow. It had obviously been raining for some time off in the mountains. Again Charlie shivered. "What if the lightening hits the river? It'll electrocute you. They'll pull your body out somewhere down in Kanawha County."

"No way. It ain't gonna happen. You think lightning has ever hit this river before?"

"I'm sure it has."

"Well, what are you worried about then? Lightning never strikes twice in the same place." Jack grinned and ran full tilt for the stream. He dove and passed into the orange water, his splash quickly hidden in the furious rainfall. He came up shaking his head like a spaniel. "C'mon in, Charlie. You weenie. It's warm as hell."

Warm sounded pretty good. Charlie, who was a little on the gangly side to begin with, looked comic as he dove in, cap, cleats, and all.

It was warm. Warm as the womb. And quiet as death. And the silty water was strangely soothing. Charlie bobbed up in time to see a bolt of lightning streak across the dark sky. The thunder was immediate, shattering, and left a clean, fresh-plowed smell in the air. The rain pounded cold against Charlie's face and he ducked under again into the warm night.

They ran into the freezing, bracing rain, screaming like banshees—the raindrops streaking their muddy faces, burning like ice—then dove from the bank again and again into the thick frothing milk. With each trip the water and the mud stimulated, then relaxed them more *and more deeply till, when the rain stopped, they lay on the sandy bank just a long breath away from sleep.*

"*You said you had something you wanted to talk about, Sampson. This had better be good, it's cost me my baseball letter.*"

"*Oh, yeah. I did say that, didn't I.*" Sampson yawned. "*I'm worried, Charlie.*"

"'*Bout what?*"

"*Everything coming apart. You know, school being over and all.*"

Charlie was smiling now and shaking his head in disbelief. "*You ain't worried about getting out of school any more than I am. Man, I'll be glad to get out of that place.*"

"*I don't mean classes and all that. I mean everything that goes with it…*"

"*You mean Libby.*"

"*Yeah.*"

"*That doesn't have to end when school ends. Stephanie and I aren't going to stop seeing each other just because school's out.*"

"*It will, though. I don't want it to, but it will. I don't mean she's going to just disappear when Nelson puts the diploma in her hand. But it's going to die. My thing with her is going to die and there is nothing I can do about it.*"

"*You're talking crazy, Jack. Libby is wild about you. Has been all along—Stephanie told me. Think about it,* man. Think about her life before you started seeing her. Nowhere. Now she's in the middle of everything."

"I'll tell you something about Libby. That stuff about being in the middle of things, that doesn't mean much to her. I mean, she likes people and all, but she's got plans, Charlie, and they're a lot bigger than being in the middle of things at Sherman High. You know what she wants to be—what she's going to do? She wants to be a singer—study voice, she calls it. She's going to school in New York for it. Her dad knows people up there and all."

"You're selling yourself short, Jack. The woman is crazy about you. Things don't just end like that."

"I appreciate you saying that, Charlie, I really do. I may not have ever told you this, but I mean it: if this thing with Libby Moss ends and that's it, at least I've gotten one thing out of the deal—the best friend I've ever had in my life. I mean that, Charlie. You must think I'm crazy, talking all the time like I do. I'll tell you, man, I've never talked to anybody the way I've talked to you. I've just had to talk about it. All this stuff that's been happening—it's wild. I'll tell you, Charlie, I woke up the other morning and I felt something that I hadn't felt since I was a little kid. I was excited to be awake. I used to wake up and wish I could go back to sleep—at least for a little while. You know, you're usually still a little sleepy. But the other day I woke up and I was just happy—just *happy to be awake, man—because I knew what a great day it was going to be. You know what I mean?"*

"Like Christmas?"

"No, it ain't like Christmas. I mean, I like Christmas as much as the next guy—and I get all psyched up about it—always have. But this is different. It's more like when you were just a little kid. Do you remember not wanting to go to sleep because you didn't want to miss anything?"

"Yeah, when I was a little guy I hated to go to bed."

"Okay, then—see if you remember this—maybe I'm wrong about this—maybe I don't really remember this—maybe I just think I do—but when I woke up a few weeks ago—it was the morning after Libby and I went out on your cycle—that night was the best time we ever had—it was perfect—you know what I mean— we sat under that big old poplar tree in the park and just stared at the shadows of the branches the moonlight made on the grass—I don't know just how to describe it—I guess it was like—I felt this is what life is supposed to be like—this is what everybody shoots for.*

"Man, it's driving me crazy trying to describe it. I feel like if I could say it—if I could put it into words—then I could hang onto it. It's like—and she didn't say this, she didn't say anything like this—it's just what I feel— it's like, you feel that this is it—this is the answer, the full satisfactory answer; everything that's gone before was just leading up to this. And that night—I don't*

*know—I felt like nothing else really matters. I mean—
here we are together and satisfied—and I don't mean
just satisfied like everything's okay, you passed the
exam or something. I mean satisfied like you don't need
anything else—you don't want anything else.*

*"The thing about that night was: I knew she felt it
too. She didn't say it, but I knew she felt it. If I've ever
known anything in my life, I know she felt it. That is
perfection, Charlie—knowing that the things you feel
and think about her—that she thinks the same about
you. It's like you could just scream 'world, you've been
wrong about me—someone understands—someone has
seen all of me and everything is okay—in fact—everything is great.' Man, you almost don't want to move
your little finger because you don't want anything to
change. You think, this is the way it's supposed to be—
this is the way I always want it to be. You know what I
mean, Charlie?"*

*"Yeah, I know exactly what you mean. I have the
same kind of feelings about Stephanie. Never ever
about anyone else. Dated Jane for nearly two years and
it wasn't like that—never thought those things with her.
I try to understand them too—try to think about them.
I'll tell you something—I heard something that I think
fits it: 'deep calleth unto deep'."*

"What does that mean?"

*"It's from the Bible. I don't know where in the Bible
or what exactly it means as far as the Bible is concerned.*

But, I just heard it—I heard it or I remembered it, I'm not sure which. It's a part of some big long thing that didn't do much for me, but when I heard that line—or remembered it—it just stuck in my mind. I kept running it over and over in my mind till it hit me. That's what's happening with us. There are things on the surface, man, ordinary things. And there are ordinary people. And then there are other things. Things that are like overwhelming. And some people see them and feel them. That's what's going on with me and Steph and you and Libby. Deep calleth unto deep."

"That's good, Charlie. That's true. Man, it's weird how the Bible keeps on popping up these days. Libby talks about the Bible sometimes...."

"But you started off about something else—something about waking up. What were you going to say?"

"Oh, yeah. I guess I did. Anyhow, I was just laying there—the alarm hadn't even gone off yet—and I felt something and it felt—I don't know—kind of familiar. It was like I told you—I was just laying there thinking how happy I was to be awake, and looking forward to the day. You're going to think I'm crazy, Charlie, but I'm going to tell you this anyway. I couldn't think of where I'd felt this feeling before, but I closed my eyes and I saw the face of a clock. It was the face of one of those old round, white wind-up alarm clocks with the bells on top. It was the clock that my mother kept outside my crib when I was a baby. I bet I haven't seen the

thing since I was three years old. But that was the clock I saw—no doubt in my mind about that. How I felt that morning was how I felt when I was a little kid waking up in the morning—it was great to be alive. The day was going to be a great adventure."

"That's wild. But that's great—I mean, she feels the same way—right?"

"No. I mean, I know she feels, or felt something. But this thing with her is over. She said so, Charlie, I might as well tell you. She told me so."

"Libby just dumped you?"

"You can't say that, Charlie. It's not like there were ever any promises made or any kind of deal. That's another thing about her. She was careful about this, Charlie. She did it right."

"Jack, there has to be an 'it' before you can say 'it's over'."

"She said she was going away to school. To New York. She didn't ask me to come see her or tell me when she would be home for the holidays or anything. She said...this'll get ya, 'You are a leader and you have incredible power. I think you are called to greatness'."

"And you're complaining about that? Sounds to me like she wants to marry you."

"I'm not complaining. But what she was saying was that both of us are called to something and they are two different things. She's going to be a singer. A

world-beating singer. Wants to write her own songs. The message is that I'm not a part of those plans."

"So what do you do?"

"I want to be part of those plans, Charlie. Whatever it costs—however long it takes. All I want is to be with her. Nothing else means much to me."

"So....what do you do?"

"That's where I'm stuck, man. I've made no plans. I've got to get something together fast and get myself on track. I can't stay around here. That's one way to make sure I never get another chance with Libby. I've got to do something, but I haven't got any great ideas."

"What about football? You could do something with that. There must have been a dozen major colleges interested in you."

"None of them liked it much when I quit before the championship game. Coach Clark quit helping me then, too. I never signed anywhere. Now it's too late."

"Come to Marshall with me. I'm walking on as a place kicker this fall. I don't have a scholarship yet, but the coach down there has been encouraging. Do it. Come with me. We could room together in the dorm. Have a blast. You'll be starting at running back before your sophomore year is over."

"Then the NFL." Sampson nodded and kept nodding, as if the thing had already happened. "We'll be playing in the NFL. Famous and rich. After the game

with the New York Giants, I'll look Libby up and that
will be it. That's what I'll do. It's a good idea, Charlie."

"I figured I owed you one. If you hadn't scored all
those touchdowns, I'd never have kicked all those
extra points."

"I got to tell you one more thing, Charlie. This
is...don't ever say anything about this to anyone..."

"That goes without saying, man."

"I know, but especially this. I feel weird even saying this."

"Yeah. Okay...whatever it is, it's safe with me."

"Charlie, the thing that's weirdest is, what if she's
right? What if all this stuff that's been happenin'—you
know—all this stuff you and I been talkin' about for
these last few weeks—ain't about us—ain't about me
and her?"

"Then it just ain't."

"Yeah, but you can't just leave it there. I could possibly be wrong about Libby. Maybe this thing with me
and her ain't meant to be. I could be wrong about that.
I don't think I am, but I could be."

"Course you could. Anybody can be wrong about
anything."

"Yeah, but if it ain't about me and her, then what's it
about?"

"Then it ain't about nothin', I guess. Why?"

"No. That's the thing, Charlie. It has got to be about
somethin'. I know I'm not wrong about that. This

stuff...all this stuff that's been happenin—the way I feel—it has to be about something. If it ain't, then nothin' is about anything."

The two were silent. Charlie sat up and stared down the river. "That is scary. Nothin' would mean anything."

"Maybe. Maybe that's it. Or maybe it's just that it all means something other than what we think it means. I don't know which is scarier, to tell you the truth. The thought of nothing meaning anything is depressing, but the other thing—that it all may mean something else—that is overwhelming to me. Because whatever it is...it's got to be...I don't know, Charlie, I just don't know."

"Hey, Jack. You know something about you and me, buddy?"

"What's that?"

"Deep calleth unto deep."

MARSHALL UNIVERSITY was a logical choice. The campus, located in Huntington, West Virginia, was only two hours away from Boone County. It was a small, state supported university and fielded a Division Two football team. Walk-ons were fairly common at Marshall, and it was not unusual for a decent lineman or special teams man to earn a spot on the roster and, then, a scholarship. Paul Anders, the head coach, had been expecting Callihan.

"All my kickers have to walk on." He told Charlie. *"You stick it out for a year, increase your range another ten yards, show me you can do the job, and we'll take care of you for your last three years."*

But Anders viewed the arrival of the heavily recruited running back with equal amounts of hope and caution. When he spoke to Sampson, it was not in his normal, robust coach's tone. Rather, he spoke softly, as if to show that Sampson's situation was not normal, he was not one of the guys and would not be treated with the regular degree of coach's abuse; as if every word was a somber, last-chance warning; as if Sampson's atonement for his reckless and disloyal behavior in high school would be a gauntlet to run; as if this chance he had been afforded was such a radical extension of grace that it should be kept as quiet as possible, so that the forces of justice would not be alerted. When he spoke, he also hurried and leaned slightly forward, fearing perhaps that the slightest slip in this act would betray the wild hope that he could not squelch, that if things worked out he would have a bona fide NFL prospect in his backfield for three seasons. *"Sampson, you've got something to show me. You've got to convince me you're committed to this program. I'm well aware of the trick you pulled on Clark in the championship game last year. That kind of stuff doesn't go around here. You'll be on the JV team this year with your buddy*

Callihan. I want to see if you've grown up enough to take this game seriously."

In the fall of 1969, Sampson and Callihan took the game seriously. Callihan put on ten pounds and was accurate from forty yards by the end of the season. Sampson found relief from the loss of Libby Moss in a single-minded devotion to his game. He was stronger than ever this year and saw this chance as a real hope. This was something he could do well if he put himself to it—maybe world-class well. People had made it to the NFL from Marshall before and it had to happen again. It had to happen to somebody and it might as well be him. This was his ticket out, his one ticket out. This new-found discipline complimenting his natural power and speed produced convincing statistics and demonstrated the kind of attitude Anders had been looking for.

After the last Junior Varsity game of the season, Anders came into the locker room. It was out of the ordinary to see the head coach in the JV locker, but Sampson saw it as a good sign.

The coach slapped Sampson on the back. "I've been watching you. Just like I said I would. And I like what I see. You've got the stuff to help us here—we all knew that, but I like your consistency. That's what I was looking for. You could have had a few great games and a few really bad ones and you wouldn't have passed the test. I want guys who play on guts, not on their mood. You played consistent this season, even when you were *hurt. That's what has done it for you. You've got a place here next season. I'm only going to recruit two other running backs 'cause I want to have plenty of room for you out there. Don't even think of getting the big head. You've got a long way to go. We played three Division One teams this year. We play four of them next year. Those guys ain't like these weak sister JV teams you've been running all over this year. All this means is that you've passed the first test. I'm willing to take a chance on you. I've changed my recruiting strategy because I'm willing to take that risk. Are you willing to make a commitment to me?"*

"Yes, sir, coach. I want to play ball for you. I want to bust some heads. Win some ball games."

The first game of Marshall University's 1970 season was at home against Furman, a conference rival. The star of that game was the halfback, Jack Sampson, with three touchdowns and 127 rushing yards. The second leading scorer was Charlie Callihan with six points: three extra points and a 34-yard field goal. The sportswriters had themselves the best kind of story—local boys make good. But that story, for this week at least, included a paragraph about Sampson's injury—an ankle. Nothing was broken, but there were some pretty bad strains and Anders didn't want him on the trip to Greenville for the game with East Carolina. It was a long trip and Jack should stick around the campus, rest up and keep on with the whirlpool. "Shoot for next week," the coach had told him. "The Citadel game is a conference game and they always play us tough."

Jack was satisfied with that. It was a long way yet from here to the NFL and the worst thing he could do was to aggravate what was now only a minor injury. As he walked to the natatorium Friday evening, he wondered at how little it had bothered him to miss the trip. Maybe his attitude was wrong. Maybe he was a little too concerned with his own health and not concerned enough about the team. He was well enough to play and well enough to help the team. He was sure of that. Funny that Anders had set him down so quickly.

The natatorium was not the centerpiece of the campus. It had been converted from an armaments warehouse just after World War II and still looked more like its first incarnation than a campus swimming pool. Consequently, other than from the swim team and a few elderly professors, the pool got almost no use. As Jack opened the door to the steamy, echoing shell, he saw that tonight was no exception. As he changed to his trunks in the empty locker room, he considered again: was there a hidden agenda in Anders' decision not to take him along? Jack had been pleased with his own performance, but with a coach you never knew. Oh, well, no sense in worrying about it now. Just work the ankle, he thought as he dove into the warm, unrippled water.

The thing that convinced Jack of his own loyalty to the team was the agonizing experience of listening to the game on the radio. They can't do anything right tonight, he thought as he heard the announcer report the team's fourth failure to make a first down in the quarter. Just three yards—that was all they needed. Third and three on their own 38. He could have gotten three yards with a dead cow strapped to his back. It was irritating.

This is how a coach must feel, he thought. All four boring quarters were agony, but when it was over, it was over, and Sampson's thoughts immediately shifted to the fact that the lackluster ground game in the 10-7 loss would undoubtedly solidify his starting role. He was no longer worried about hidden agendas. The guys would be glad to have him back, they would realize how important he was to the team, that his performance in the first game had been no fluke. And the defense had played pretty well. Next week he'd be back, they would play at home, and things would be different.

Jack flipped off the radio and looked at the clock on his dormroom desk. It was not even six-o-clock yet. He'd spent enough time in this deserted dormitory and he wasn't going to suffer through another weekend cafeteria dinner. He was going to The Buffalo. Time for some good old-fashioned drive-in food for a change. He shuffled through his desk drawer for cash. Four dollars and thirty-seven cents—enough money for three burgers.

The Buffalo was just a couple of blocks off campus. It was a mom and pop joint that had started nearly twenty years ago as a drive-in but now did most of its business in its tiny dining room. By now, Jack Sampson was a regular there.

"Whacha doin' here? No wonder we lost the ball-game." Ed White owned The Buffalo and was a diehard fan in the best tradition of college-town joint-owners. He had covered the walls of his place with photographs of great moments in Marshall sports. The faded black-and-whites matched the overall dinginess of the place.

"Hurt. Tore my ankle up a little bit last game. Coach wanted me to stay off it."

"Don't look to me like you're stayin' off it."

"Come on, Eddie. Give me a break. I'll be back out there next week. I'll score a touchdown for you."

"Whatcha havin' Jackie? You want a burger—Buffalo Burger?"

The promise of the touchdown was the kind of thing Ed White lived for and it meant that Jack Sampson did not have to pay for the three Buffalo Burgers he inhaled that evening. This left him with four dollars and thirty-seven cents in his pocket.

He could not, even in his newfound discipline, force himself to study tonight. There was plenty to do. There was always plenty to do, but he sensed he must pace himself somewhat to be able to sustain his drive to the top. Studying on Saturday night was too much, it was burnout speed. Besides, he couldn't bring himself to go back to the nearly deserted dormitory.

Four dollars would get him into the movie, but going to the theater alone was no fun. He would feel self-conscious standing in the ticket-line alone, surrounded by high-school kids on dates. He headed for the arcade. It would be empty and if he was on his game, the four bucks and change would keep him going for several hours and get him tired enough to go to sleep.

He ended the evening at midnight, as the arcade closed, with a dollar and twelve cents left over. He found himself picking up the pace during the walk back to the dorm, pulling his neck into the collar of his jacket like a turtle. It was amazing how quickly it could get chilly this time of year. He topped a little ridge and the dormitory came into view, a tower of windows, few of them lit. It was late and the team was out of town.

He saw a girl leave the building and begin walking in his direction. She was a silent shadow slipping in and out of the light circles from the street lamps in the distance. She walked with a relaxed confidence which intrigued him. He immediately sensed that she was coming to him, although she was too far away to recognize, and there was nothing familiar in her walk or dress. She came directly toward him and he saw her face. She was a small girl—short and slender, probably a freshman, someone who roomed in the other tower of the dormitory. Her complexion was flawless and she wore a hooded wool jacket and blue-jeans stuffed into cordovan riding boots. He did not recognize her; now he was sure of that. He had never seen her before and, if this gal had been staying at the dorm, she would not have gone unnoticed. She did not slow her deliberate pace as she approached him—not even as she spoke with a voice he had never heard and would never hear again.

"Are you Jack Sampson?" she asked.

"Yeah, that's me." Jack stopped. It would be nice to talk with somebody. She looked like a nice somebody.

But the girl did not slow down. In fact, she had passed Sampson completely before she finished her last, brief statement. "Your mother wants you to call her. It's very important." And she walked on.

That was the first odd thing. Another was that all the night security posts were unmanned as he walked into the common areas of the dorm. There was no one at the front desk. He had never seen that before.

It was late to be calling home, and he wasn't sure about the validity of the message he had gotten from the girl, but maybe something was wrong. If nothing was wrong the worst of it would be that he would wake his mother up. An unexpected call this late in the night would scare her at first, but she would get over that quickly and be happy to hear from her only son. On the other hand, if the message was for real, not making the call would be a big mistake. Jack Sampson knew the message was for real when his mother answered her phone at 12:34 a.m. on the first ring.

"Jack?" She sounded desperate, her voice was almost a gasp.

"Mom...yeah, it's me. It's Jack."

Now she went completely out of control. She spoke in half sentences, punctuated with sobs. "You're okay. You're okay. You're okay..."

"Yeah, mom. I'm fine. What's wrong? What did you think happened to me?"

"Oh, honey, you don't know?" Here there was an extended pause. When Mrs. Sampson spoke again, everything about her voice had changed. She spoke slowly now and in a tone that had changed from panic to deep sympathy. "Oh, honey. Don't you know? The plane crashed, honey. The team plane. Something went wrong. They couldn't land. It ran into a hillside out near the airport. They think everyone has been.... Jack, are you alone, honey?"

It was, and is, the biggest sports-related disaster in American history. There were seventy-five people on the plane: the entire varsity team, except Jack Sampson, the entire varsity coaching staff, the cheerleading squad, the university athletic director and his wife, the team physician and his wife, and a few supporters.

There were no survivors.

A LUMP of lead. A big lump of lead at the bottom of his stomach. It was a weight that pushed against his guts and never went away. It was real. So real that he considered going to the doctor to have something done about it. But that was a delusion—just wishful thinking. If there really was anything down there it would have come up by now. Six days after the crash and he had not gone a night without vomiting. Besides, he knew this feeling. He had had it before—after the explosion at Catton. He had carried that lead ball around for months. This sensation was the only exception to an overall numbness. He lived reflexively—he walked to class, he carried a notebook, but took no notes. He ate, but he did not taste.

His psychology teacher, Mr. Williams, saw it. "You're not making it in this class, Jack. That is quite understandable. But it will do you no good at all for me to ignore this problem and just pass you even though you aren't meeting course requirements. There are people here on campus who can help you. Some of the best people in the country are here now just to help people who have been affected like you. I sympathize with you, Jack. Believe me, there is no one on campus who hasn't been affected in some way by this terrible thing."

He would not go to therapy. Therapy was for people who imagined things. What could it do for him—convince him that he had imagined this? He felt as is he had very little of himself left and he was not about to trust anyone's—expert or not—tampering with it. He would not go home, either. Charlie would not be there. There would be no Libby Moss, and never anyone like her there again. What would be there would be that river. That dirty, frozen river. He would not go back there. He did not know where he would go, but he would not go back there.

In 1970, the United States government performed a service for young men who did not know where they wanted to go: the government chose for them—Viet Nam.

In Viet Nam, especially in the years just before the American withdrawal, numbness was a great asset to an enlisted man. It was the only way one could keep his sanity and it was cultivated by the conscripted soldiers. Sampson went to Viet Nam numb and, in eighteen months, returned decorated and numb.

THESE THINGS were the chapters of Jack Sampson's past. These were the things that rushed through his mind as he sat on the rock with R.L. Maddux, who had just asked him to take on leadership of the UMWA local. In accepting, he would tie himself forever to this dying place.

"JACK," MADDUX continued, "don't shirk this. You're a born leader. You're strong. Naturally strong."

Maddux stood now and turned to spit tobacco juice. Then he looked back down at Sampson. Maddux knew exactly how much he was asking, and it pained him to ask so much of anyone. "You're a good man, but people are always a little afraid of you. That's what you've got to have for a job like this. You can get these men motivated. You can stand up to the damn companies. You are what the union needs now, but if you won't let me get you on before my time passes, this new bunch won't even have the sense to know they need you."

Jack Sampson ended his reverie and came to himself. Here was R.L.Maddux asking a question he had every right to ask. Yet, it didn't seem right. Here was the baton, the flaming baton of power. This was Elijah's mantle, the staff of Moses. It was a symbol of struggle against awesome odds; behind it were years of beastlike toil, sacrifice of every kind and measure, and ragged battle. Its passing should be a high moment. The one who received it should tremble at the honor and the responsibility that accompanied it.

Jack knew he should feel these things, but he did not feel them. The answer in his throat was a simple refusal: *I don't think this fits with my plans right now.* He could hear himself say it and he could see the shock and disappointment on Maddux's face. He did not want to see that disappointment. Besides that, this reason would be false: he had no plans. How could he say that anything did or did not fit into them?

It was a bad thing to accept this half-heartedly, but it would be worse to say no. He could not say no. He would accept, perhaps the heart for it would follow. What else was he going to do anyway?

"I'll do it, R.L. When's the election?"

PART Three

1987

19

"Mance Grayley is a hick. That's why the union ain't done no good in the last four years." Sam Dawson, who railed at the little group, was also a hick.

Sampson, who was rocked back in a folding chair and staring into the wall, hated Dawson. He hated Dawson's dirty-blonde hair, which was wiry and tightly curled and clung to his scalp like a tight helmet. He hated Dawson's belly, which hung over his belt and quivered when Dawson ranted and raved, which was most of the time. The ranting and raving was what Sampson hated most of all.

Sampson had known Dawson since elementary school and had been tired of Dawson since elementary school. Dawson was the kind of guy who had always griped about everything, from an umpire's call to the service in a restaurant. It usually got him nowhere, inasmuch as his claims were usually as senseless as they were loud, but every dog has its day.

Dawson had made his way in as president of UMWA Local 1254 by ranting and raving for which there was, these days, a ready market. The last three contracts had been far from satisfactory: wages had not kept pace with inflation, and health benefits had eroded substantially. Maddux had been on the money about the new generation of miner. They showed no insight into the situation and displayed no will to fight. They just didn't like the way things were going. Rhetoric had always had an important place in the struggle of the union. What the newcomers did not seem to understand was that rhetoric had to be based on something—it had to have a basis.

That basis had to be a moral basis and it had to be discovered or, at least, it had in the past been discovered, through struggle and suffering. Maddux had said it another way: "The workin' man don't win because of power or because of money. And he certainly don't win because the other side is weak. If you're going to win, you got to know you're right. When you know that...even when you know that...you cain't just go to battle, you got to go to war."

It seemed to Sampson that somewhere along the line, as Maddux had suspected, not being completely pleased with a result had taken the place of "knowin' you're right." Ranting was easy and seemed like the right thing to do. Thus, when discontentment took the place of righteous indignation, Sam Dawson was in his glory. There was no one around who could hold a candle to Sam when it came to expressing discontentment.

Sampson's first campaign for Local president began with the allegation that Mance Grayley, the national president, had sold out. This met with little approval. As shallow as the new troops were, and as seemingly ineffective as Grayley's administration had been, the charge of treason would not stick. Grayley had paid his dues: he had thirty years underground and could not go for five minutes without coughing the loose, rattling hack which was the unmistakable mark of black-lung disease. Whatever else he was, Mance Grayley was one of them. He talked like them, he looked like them, and there was at least one member left in nearly every local who had known him personally, or at least knew some of his extensive family, all of whom still lived, very modestly, in the coalfields.

But there was something wrong. The union was failing in negotiations, so there must be something wrong with the national presidency. It was Timothy Tagliani, candidate for the national presidency of the UMWA, who gave Sam Dawson the right something to whine about. Tagliani had just made his first campaign speech in the state of West Virginia. Dawson found him later in a corner of the hall and showed his interest. "I've been telling these people Grayley needs to go, but they won't listen to me. I don't know what to say to them. He's killing us and they're all in love with him."

Tagliani leaned toward Dawson and put his arm around Dawson's wide shoulders. "Grayley is a hick," Tagliani whispered. "He means well, but he has no education, no sophistication, no street smarts. That's obvious to people like you and me. The day of the earnest country boy at the negotiating table is over.

"The companies hire people specially trained to do their negotiating for them. Most of them are lawyers. Some are psychologists. Mance Grayley is a sheep among wolves. He'll get taken to the cleaners every time...just like he always has."

It was quite a ploy—to take Grayley's source of strength—his commonness, his similarity to the rank and file member—and use it against him. The young members didn't see it coming. They were sophisticated enough to understand Tagliani's argument and not aware enough of their own identity to be offended by it. Or perhaps it was that they shared no identity with Grayley. After all, Grayley was a soldier, they were heirs.

"I tell you, this union will fall apart if Grayley is elected again." Dawson walked around the room as he raved, looking, in turn, at each of the five Local presidents. "Tagliani is the man and we need to support him. We need to get the word out to the rank-and-file that Tagliani is the only guy who can keep up with the company crooks."

Sampson shook his head. It was truly a sad day when you were down to agreeing with Sam Dawson, but as much as Sampson hated to admit it, Dawson was right: the union had failed in negotiations in the last four years running, and Grayley was a very unsophisticated man. Tagliani was educated and seemed sincere. He had certainly done his homework before meeting Jack Sampson.

"I have looked forward to meeting you, Jack. I know your reputation. I know about your father. And I know there isn't a more influential union man in this county. In your case, that's how it ought to be. I want to tell you about my ideas for this union. I think you'll like them. I certainly hope you do. I'm going to need your support in this election. Grayley still has a lot of support and this place right here—this county and the ones surrounding it—is his real stronghold. I may not win here, no matter what, but I need to show well. I need votes here, Jack."

Tagliani's ideas for the union—at least the version he offered Sampson—had a lot to do with Jack Sampson. He said a mistake the union had always made was failing to make full use of its leadership talent at the grassroots level. There were lots of Locals around the country—in Tennessee and Wyoming, for example—which did not have strong leadership. Tagliani would have a few lieutenants in his cabinet who could be dispatched to such areas in a crises. People who knew how to deal with the companies on a local level and, perhaps more importantly, people who could inspire trust and confidence in the national administration.

He wanted Sampson as one of those lieutenants—probably for the top lieutenant post. He felt like he would need Sampson if the program was to work. Of course, this would mean that Sampson would have to spend a lot of his time at national headquarters in New York City. Tagliani understood that Jack had no family commitments that would make such an arrangement inconvenient.

New York City.

It only made sense. He had been told time and again that his gift was leadership—that he had a destiny to fulfill. That had to happen somewhere—anywhere but here. Anywhere but Boone County, West Virginia. It had taken him a long time to figure that out. He had thought maybe too long, but here was a chance—a late-blooming chance. He would support Tagliani even though Tagliani would lose here. He would be hurting himself with the local miners, but something had to give.

So Sampson sat rocked back in the folding chair as Dawson railed on. It seemed silly; everyone in the room—all six of the Local presidents—was already aligned. There would be no more conversions to the Tagliani camp. Sampson had already made his one and only successful campaign pitch to the man who was seated next to him: John Helton. As a result of Sampson's repeated urgings, Helton had finally agreed to support Tagliani.

20

Sampson sat deeply in a frayed, upholstered chair looking across the wide room of the Local Union Hall at the two men in suits. It was near dusk and the naked concrete floor and cinderblock walls were giving back the heat of the day. The smell of coming rain wafted through the screenless open windows. The men in suits looked alternatively at newspapers and at their watches. A grey metal table stood in a corner of the room; alone on the table stood a locked metal box with a thin slot in its top.

"I got it's time," said one of the men. He did not look up.

"He'll be here," said Sampson.

The man did not look at Sampson but jerked his newspaper back open. The rustle of the pages echoed in the room.

Sampson stood and walked closely past the two men and out of the door, onto the gravel lot. The men did not look up at Sampson as he passed. Outside, the smell of rain coming was stronger and Sampson walked out onto the dirt road and looked down the hollow at the little stretch of highway visible through the oaks and at the cars and pickups that passed now and then. He raked one boot back and forth, rattling the gravel. The sky was grey with clouds now, the breeze whipping up, and dark

coming on fast. He walked back toward the white cinderblock Hall, toward the doorway and a bulletin board
that hung under a lamp outside the door. He stared for a
while at the ragged papers tacked onto the board.

The rain started. It came at first in quick, blown
spurts or sheets rat-tatting against the window glass
and then gone. Then the wind gusted cold, then ceased.
Then the rain came hard, relentless and driving.

Sampson ducked under the small awning above the
doorway. He looked at his watch and into the Hall at the
two men who still sat at their papers. Then he heard the
car engine in the hollow and saw its headlight beams,
bright streaks in the shadows of the wet-leaved oaks.

The car came fast up the hollow, the rain visible in its
lights and its windshield wipers working furiously and
its radio blaring.The car stopped at the edge of the road
and the empty gravel lot, fifteen yards away from the
Hall. A short, fat, bearded young man stepped out. He
was wearing a too small tee-shirt and a too tight baseball cap from under which his hair, shoulder-length and
uncombed, stuck out in curls and waves as if itself alive
and flexed in a desperate attempt at escape.

"It's about damn time," said Sampson.

The man, who was looking at Sampson, did not
respond.

"Why did you park clear over in Logan County? You
tryin' to get exercise? You know it's rainin', John?"

The man at first did not respond, but walked slowly in the rain, his belly jiggling. Behind him the windshield wipers were still pumping, the radio still blaring. He walked past Sampson. His t-shirt was already soaked and it clung to his torso. He reeked of whiskey.

"Let's just get it done, man." He walked under the little porch awning and went dripping into the Hall with Sampson behind him. The two men in suits were already standing.

"I'm John Helton; here for the ballots."

"We'll need to look at your card," said one of the men.

"It's him," said Sampson.

Helton's wallet was long and black and chained to a belt loop. He pulled it from his rear pocket, fished out a card and handed it to the man. The other man was across the room. He took a clipboard from the top of a file cabinet and began walking back toward the other men. As he passed by the big window facing the lot, the hail started. It came hard and all at once, as if at the forthwith command of the god of the storm. The man stopped at the big window as the hail pelted hard on the roof of the Hall and clattered loudly against the parked car. In a moment the white pellets were mounded into lines and arcs surrounding the ambits of the moving wipers.

"Damn," he said.

Helton signed the paper on the clipboard and went to the table and tried lifting the ballot box with one hand.

"You boys must'a had a good turn-out."

Helton lifted the box with both hands and started to the door, tilting with the weight of the box. As he approached the door, Sampson reached a hand toward the box-handle.

"Here," he said. "Give you a hand."

Helton jerked the box away from Sampson, staggering backward with the swing of the heavy box.

"Get the hell away. That ain't procedure."

Helton pushed the door open with his back and lumbered into the gravel lot, now white with hail pellets. The high and hollow sound of the hail against the ballot box added to the chorus of hail sounds. He rested the box on the chrome rear bumper, steadying it with his thigh, and took a key from his pocket and opened the trunk. Helton's hand on the key followed the trunk lid into the air and when he was thus stretched he shifted his leg and the ballot box slipped on the wet chrome bumper and fell, corner first, onto his foot. Helton fell to his back on the lot and rolled side to side in the hailstones and made loud oaths. Sampson trotted from under the porch awning to behind the car. The hail was already collecting in Helton's hair.

"Get away," Helton screamed. "Get the hell away."

The ballot box was lying on its front in the hail and Sampson lifted it to the gaping trunk of the car. He looked inside the trunk, which was illumined, and saw five other ballot boxes. The top of each box bore red stenciling. Two of the boxes were labeled "Local 1219," two "Local 2430," and one, already in the trunk, bore a label identical to that box now in his hands, "Local 2131." Sampson dropped the box into the trunk and looked back at the Hall. The men in suits were not on the gravel lot or under the awning. He moved to the side of the car and tried to see into the big window of the Hall but he did not see the men. He went back behind the car and stood over Helton, who was in a fetal position on his side, holding his foot in his hands.

"You think that hurts, you son-of-a-bitch?" Sampson asked. Sampson rared and kicked Helton in the buttocks, moving Helton's whole body inches up in the hail and gravel. "What kind of funny shit is this?" Sampson stepped back and then forward and kicked him again and Helton began to plead and to cry.

"Don't Jack. Don't kill me."

"Just get in the car." Sampson was shaking as he yelled. "Get in that damn car and get the hell out of here now."

Helton crawled to the car and pulled himself inside, the radio louder as he opened the door. He shifted into gear and as the car began to move Sampson kicked the door, rocking the car and leaving a deep dent. Helton did not move and looked straight ahead as he drove. The car turned and headed back down the hollow, its trunk still agape and the trunk lid waving up and down with the bumps in the road like a laughing mouth.

Sampson went back into the Hall. The men were sitting around a desk at the back of the wide room. One of them was on the telephone. The other looked up at Sampson and spoke.

"Everything okay?"

"Yeah."

21

There was no sign yet of dawn when Mark Varner drove the cruiser out of the barracks lot. He drove west through Bandy where the little cluster of houses showed only a few lit windows, and drove through the switch-backs up Tallory Mountain and away from the Walhonde Valley. The road turned northwest three miles out of Bandy and into a hollow and there followed the railroad along Len's Creek. At Prenter Station the road left the creek and turned northeast and up Drawdy Mountain and came out of the trees at the mountaintop and there he saw in the rear-view mirror the sky above the ridge to the east pink with dawn. From Drawdy's ridge he dropped back into a narrow hollow at the bottom of which he crossed Short Creek on a makeshift bridge twenty yards downstream from the ruined bridge. The road started back up the other side of the hollow, then turned east and out of the hollow into a narrow valley where the road followed the Little Coal River into Procious, Madison, and Danville, all shambles of storefronts close against the crooked streets and the highway.

At Danville he stopped at the traffic light and turned right up Bull Mountain. Near the ridge he turned onto the entrance of the four-lane Corridor entering that highway northbound. There was light traffic in the southbound lanes, pickups and tractor-trailers all still using headlights.

He drove north along the four-lane, through the long shadows the mountains cast west in the rising sun. As he neared the mountaintops, he passed between the highwalls of terraced sandstone, stair-steps each thirty feet high and eight feet deep, slanting and terracing away from the bed of the highway and up to the ridges. The pitched planes of stone were marked top to bottom at regular intervals with perfect vertical grooves, the remnants of drill-holes where charges had been sunk and tamped and exploded in precise order and measure as the road crews had brought the mountains low and, with the stuff of those mountains, exalted the valleys.

He was doing eighty-five in the cruiser with no other car in sight, the only sound the white noise of the engine and the almost regular bleat of the tires over the seams in the pavement. Twenty miles from Charleston he crossed over a ridge; the valley ahead was pasture bounded north and south by mountainsides that were cleared halfway up and fenced. A herd of white-faced cattle dotted the valley to his left and on the far mountainside.

Varner saw a flicker of light on the tree line of the far mountainside. He could not tell what had caused the glimmer, or whether it was his imagination. Then, just below that tree line a hawk soared. Everywhere in the valley was the silence of its flight. It glided to the east in a line so true as to prove its total independence from the earth, and that it drew no bearing from its shadows of turning nor from any fallen and imperfect thing. It was so distant as to be barely perceptible to Varner. He squinted and dropped his foot from the gas and the hawk seemed stationary in the air and all that moved was the earth and the things of man and the things that will perish and the earth moved on its axis and the cruiser coasted north and all things moved away until the hawk was nothing to them but a shimmer in the sunlight.

The Corridor ended as it entered the Kanawha Valley at Marmet and there he turned west and drove along the highway on the south rim of the broad valley. He looked down and across the valley on the chemical plants, intricate mazes of pipes, stacks, and tanks, and the coal-loading docks on the riverbanks and at the river itself, green and wide. As he came out of a long bend in the road, the valley opened to the north and he saw the city. On the east end were the neighborhoods—houses, streets, gas stations and churches and on the north bank mansions—old brick structures with tile roofs and archways, tall windows, gazebos and long, level lawns bounded by huge oaks, stretching down to the riverbank and docked pleasure boats.

In the distance the tall buildings downtown glistened in the sun. There was no shadow now on this east-facing side of the city, and the buildings in this clear brightness appeared as perfect geometric shapes without blemish.

The city looked benign and simplified, like a city in a child's picture book.

He drove into the downtown and down Quarrier Street. The shops were not yet open and there was little traffic. Two blocks from the Federal Building he stopped at a red light and a man and woman in sweat-suits ran past the cruiser and across the empty intersection against the red light without so much as a look around.

He pulled the cruiser onto the parking lot behind the Federal Building. The blacktopped lot was almost empty behind the mechanical gate arm. As he entered the lot a young woman in jeans and a sweater came out from the rear door. She was holding a large ring of keys in her hand and she walked onto the lot and toward the gate-arm and motioned to Varner to approach. He drove to the arm and rolled down the window.

"You're Sally Thomas, I take it."

"Yep."

She took a card from the front pocket of her jeans, inserted it into a receptacle and pulled it back out. The gate made a clanking sound like metal expanding in heat; when the guard arm went up Varner drove past it and into the lot.

"Anywhere?" Varner yelled back to the young woman.

"Anywhere but four-twenty-six. Judge Carson comes in on Saturdays sometimes."

Varner parked the car and reached into the glove compartment and took out a tape cassette and got out of the car and walked toward Sally Thomas, holding the tape just below his chin with his left hand and tapping it conspicuously with his right index. finger. She nodded her head and smiled and they walked to the door of the Federal Building. She was tall and neat and smelled of citrus. She again used the plastic card and the glass double doors to the building swung open.

Mark Varner and Sally Thomas sat across from each other at a glass-topped walnut table in a room without windows. A tape player was on the table between them and they both wore headsets. Sally Thomas had before her a legal pad. Her eyes were closed and into the room where there were no ears to hear she mouthed the word *there*. She stopped the tape, rewound it a moment, then again pushed play. The two listened silently, all the time Sally Thompson's eyes shifting from her notes, to the tape machine, to the ceiling, closing for long moments, all the time Varner's eyes fixed on her, the unknown. Sally Thomas again stopped the machine and removed her headset and nodded at Varner.

"Let's talk about it," she said.

Varner took off his headset and laid it on the table.

"Is this guy as dangerous as he sounds?"

"I think he is," said Varner.

"You think he killed Maddux."

"Yeah. He's in on it some way."

"Is Tonya scared of him?"

"Yes."

"What's she going to do?"

"I don't know. I don't know from day to day what she's going to do."

Sally Thomas spoke slowly, weighing each word. "Well, there's a case here. This tape's enough to convict him on the drug charge. But Tonya will have to testify. She'll have to get on the stand and authenticate this tape at the very least. Is she willing to do that?"

"I told her up front that she'd have to do that. She understood. But whether she'll come through or not, that's another story."

"I need to talk to her. Can you get her in here?"

"I don't know. It's hard for her to get away from him for any length of time. She's got a baby, too. And, even if we could work it out somehow, I can't guarantee that she'd want to. She is hard to deal with. She gets her kicks out of making life difficult for me."

"He gets only a year or two at most on this. Even if we win on everything. That really won't do the trick here. It's not enough to get Tonya any room. I wouldn't blame her for not testifying under these conditions."

Varner shrugged and lifted his hands, palms up. "Just subpoena her. What's she going to say? That's not me on the tape? She'll have to give us the bare necessities. I don't mean to be hardhearted about it, but we can't just let this go."

Sally Thomas shook her head slowly. "She doesn't have to testify at all—subpoena or not. As long as they are married, she has the absolute right to refuse to give any testimony against him. She has to do it voluntarily."

"What about just putting the tape in? I could identify the voices—say I got the tape from her."

"I can't rule that out as a possibility, but it would be very unusual. I don't want to indict Dawson on the assumption that we will succeed in getting the tape into evidence without her. I want a witness to the conversation."

Sally Thomas lifted her legal pad and looked over the pages of notes. "Have you talked to her since Maddux was killed?"

"No. I don't even know if she's still alive, to tell you the truth."

Sally Thomas did not respond. She continued to study the notes.

"I need to make an arrest," said Varner.

She nodded her head, but did not look up. "I know," she said. "Is there anything on the Maddux murder yet?"

"No. Ballistics early next week, maybe. But that's not much without a suspect. I don't look for that to move any faster than this has."

"We've got grand jury here next week. Think you could get Tonya in for that?"

"I could try."

She laid the pad back on the table before her and put the cap back onto a plastic pen and laid the pen across the pad. "She could still back out at trial, even if we get her testimony tied down in the grand jury. It's kind of a bluff, but it's better than not doing it, I guess. I really want to talk to her, get a feel for her. Maybe a subpoena would help to get her in here."

"I think I can manage that." Varner said. "I'll get her served and get her in here if it's humanly possible. But, I need to make an arrest, Sally. I don't want to be over dramatic about this, but they're shooting at me. At least they thought they were. Whoever shot Maddux thought they were getting me."

"I know that. I can't believe they left you down there without a partner." She looked at the ceiling. "That is crazy. Give me the lawsuit for the cop who gets hurt in a situation like yours," Sally rolled her eyes. "Lawyer's early retirement."

Varner glanced down at the pager attached to his belt. He removed the black plastic square and held it in his left hand between his thumb and forefinger and lifted it halfway to his face. Seven digits spread across the tiny screen. He looked at Sally Thomas.

"It's her," he said. "Tonya Dawson just paged me. I need a phone."

She led him down a hallway. They passed by one open office door after another on the outer side of the hall. Rectangles of light lay across the hall carpet at the open doors. In one office a young man was sitting on the floor amid layers of documents speaking into a dictating machine he held in his hand. Sally Thomas stepped into an office and motioned to Varner to come in. She shut the door behind them.

"Phone's on my desk. Can I listen in?"

"It's fine with me, but if she senses anything she'll go crazy. I'm telling you, there's nobody like her."

"Don't use the speaker phone. Just let me hear her if you can."

Varner punched the number and stared at the walls of Sally Thomas's office—diplomas, her wedding picture, a co-ed softball team picture cut from a newspaper and a courtroom artist's pastel rendering of Sally Thomas in a blue suit standing at a podium before a jury.

"Hello."

Varner nodded at Sally Thomas. "Hello Tonya," he said.

"Where are you?"

"That doesn't matter. I'm not far…"

"Don't you tell me what matters. I know what matters."

"I'm not very far away, Tonya. That's all I was going to say."

Varner held the receiver away from his ear and waved Sally Thomas closer to the phone. Tonya Dawson's voice was audible everywhere in the office.

"I know where you are. You're in Charleston. You think I'm stupid?"

Varner did not respond.

"What are you doing?" she demanded.

"Police business."

"Smartass. I thought we was in this together. I tell you everything. You don't tell me nothin'. I thought you was going to protect me. Do you have any idea what I'm going through? What it's like to live with him? What if he would find out?"

Varner lowered his voice. "What's he doing, Tonya? What's he done, now?"

"Only about killed me, that's all. He got drunk again last night, came home screaming at me."

"Are you hurt?"

"Nothing more than usual. I'll make it."

"What was he yelling about, Tonya?"

"Wouldn't you like to know?"

With his empty hand Varner pointed to the receiver, frowned and shook his head at Sally Thomas. She was making notes on a legal pad, but acknowledged his gesture.

"Yeah, I would like to know and I don't want to play games with you."

"Don't you tell me games. You know what you promised me."

"I know. I'll keep my promises if you keep yours."

"You promised a lot."

"What was he yelling about last night?"

"He said he was going to be caught."

"Caught for what?"

"Caught over killing Helton. Do you know more than you've told me?"

Varner looked at Sally Thomas who was wide-eyed. She made quick horizontal cylinders in the air with her open hand, encouraging Varner to continue.

"What did he say?"

"You're in too big a hurry."

"We'd better hurry, Tonya. People are getting shot. What did he say?"

"He said somebody is talking. He knows somebody is talking."

"How does he know?"

"I don't know how he knows."

"What did he say, Tonya. How did he say he knew this?"

"Nothin'. I can't remember it. I can't remember everything."

"Think about it, Tonya. You have to remember. People's lives could depend on it. Your life could depend on it."

"I was upset, damn it. I can't remember everything. I'm not sure what all he said. And you're pushing too hard on me. You never act nice to me. Would that kill you—to just be nice once in a while? Everything's on the tape."

Sally Thomas clenched and shook her left fist.

"You taped him?"

"Ever bit of it. If this machine of yours worked, then it's all on there. I had the thing turned on."

"God bless you."

"That's a little more like it."

"I need that tape, Tonya. As soon as I can get it. Can I get it from you today?"

"If you're ever going to get it, you're going to have to get it today. Sam will be back here in a few minutes. He just ran out to the store. He's got picket duty tonight at eight. You come here after then. I can't guarantee you anything after tonight. And you come by yourself. And you'd better be ready to be real nice to me."

"Okay. I'll be there at eight—a little after eight."

Varner replaced the phone and looked at Sally Thomas. She was grinning.

"Can you have it here tomorrow? We need to get it transcribed right away. I want a transcript before we do the arrest. I'll want to play the tape for the grand jury, too."

"That's no problem. If I get the tape, it'll be here first thing tomorrow morning.

"What's this *if* business?"

"You just never know with her."

"Take a subpoena. I'll get you a subpoena right now. We'll haul her in front of the grand jury. That'll cut the games."

Varner did not respond. He stood up and stepped toward the door of the office.

22

Varner drove an unmarked cruiser to the top of Poplar Ridge. The dirt road wound up the mountainside through big timber, followed the ridge for half a mile, then wound back down into Big Horse Creek Hollow. On top of the ridge, Varner stopped the cruiser at a wide place where the power line right-of-way crossed the road. He drove the car off the road and into the high grass of the right-of-way and parked it at the edge, by a stand of pines, and walked across the road to the west side of the ridge. The west-facing side of the mountain had been clear cut and was covered with weeds, brambles and sumac, all brittle and gold and brown with autumn. The view west and into Big Horse Creek Hollow was unobstructed. It was six forty-five and the sun was slipping behind Drawdy Mountain.

He looked away to the west and into the sun above the ridge. A strong breeze lifted out of the hollow below, bending the knee-high grass and, across the hollow, stirring the dead leaves still on the trees covering the opposite mountainside. The rustle started as a whisper and built, as it climbed the mountain, to a shivering crescendo.

Varner shaded his eyes with his hand. His shadow was long behind him, across the grass and dirt road all yellow in the late afternoon sunlight.

He looked into the hollow. There, in the distance, Dawson's trailer, Camaro, and half-ton Chevy pickup were strewn among the weeds and brush without apparent intentional arrangement, like things that had been tossed.

At six fifty-two Varner saw the trailer door open and Sam Dawson walk onto the front stoop. Varner took a step back from the edge of the ridge. He saw the door close behind Dawson and then he heard it close. The sun had begun to dip behind Drawdy Mountain to the west and the forested east-facing ridge opposite Varner had gone from brilliant autumn reds and yellows to grey shadow. The bottom of the hollow was dark now and Dawson, wearing camouflage fatigues and carrying what appeared to be a lunch-pail, started the truck and drove it down the crooked ruts beside the trailer and onto the dirt road and down into the hollow and into the shadow of the mountain.

Varner started back across the ridge and in the middle of the road he crouched and looked toward the spot where he had parked the car and into the cleared power right-of-way.

By the time Dawson's truck passed by the power right-of-way, Dawson was using his headlights. That close canvas of sky that minutes ago had vibrated with the brilliant oils of autumn had vanished and the sky, new with night, was muted watercolor grey and a cool moon and single star reigned in that vacant and far-away thing.

Varner watched the truck's taillights disappear over the ridge and started the car and moved it slow and bouncing with the ruts out of the right-of-way and onto the ridge road. He did not turn on the headlights.

The moon was nearly full and the dust of the road seemed to soak up its light and give it back in controlled measure. The road surface before him was luminous and appeared to float as a thin layer just above the solid earth. He drove down the ridge and out of a switchback and saw the trailer. No light in any window. Forty yards above the trailer he pulled to the side of the road and killed the engine and watched the trailer and listened.

Varner did not see the figure emerge from the shadows deep in the hollow. He did not see the man until the man was within a few yards of the trailer. The man was walking fast, taking long strides through the high grass, and heading for the trailer door. As the man approached the front of the trailer, he was obscured from Varner's view. Varner took his pistol from under his seat and stuffed it under his belt. He unscrewed the plastic covering on the dome light in the ceiling of the cruiser and removed the bulb. He pulled the door-handle slowly, inch by inch, until the door released and he slowly cracked the door and nursed it open enough to slip out of the car. He did not close the door. He had taken just three crouched steps toward the trailer when he heard the gunshots.

Three shots, and each of the three lit up the trailer windows. Varner squatted at the front fender of his car. The man came back into sight. He was running very fast back into the depth of the hollow, back into the shadow. Varner stood, then ducked again as the trailer lights came on. He heard loud music coming from the trailer. Screaming rock music. He remained in a crouch and started toward the trailer. He was twenty feet from the rear window of the trailer and prone in the weeds when through the window he saw Tonya Dawson. She was naked and held a back revolver in her left hand and a joint in her right hand. She was dancing, lifting her hands high, writhing to the crazy music. Her eyes were unfocused and she made loud utterances in an unknown tongue. Her voice was that of an old and angry man.

23

Varner stood in a phone booth on a cinder lot outside a gas station that was closed for the night. The cruiser was parked beside the booth. The engine was off and the lights were off. Varner, holding the phone receiver to his ear, stepped outside; the light inside the booth went out as he opened the door. He held his other hand over his other ear and spoke in a low voice.

"I don't know who it was. I'd say Jack Sampson, but I'm pretty prejudiced in that matter right now. And that's just a guess, really. He was big enough to have been Sampson."

"What did you do?" asked Sally Thomas.

"When I saw Tonya with the gun, I got out of there. She was stoned out of her gourd, and she thought she had shot at me. She was wanting to get me, no question."

"What are you going to do?"

"I'm not going back there without a warrant. I've got to make an arrest. We've got to put somebody in jail and cool things down."

"Who can we arrest?"

"How about Dawson?"

"Tonya?"

"No. Sam Dawson. Arrest him on the drug stuff. The tape we just listened to."

"There are problems with that case, Mark. We'd have all kinds of problems at trial. Big problems."

"I'm having big problems right now."

"The case isn't ready. I don't like to arrest before the case is ready to go. I've made that mistake before."

"We can work the case up after the arrest."

"Oh, no. No, sir. Done that, too. It's just a mess. You get counsel in the case right away and they're looking over your shoulder every minute. They start filing things that I'll have to respond to; they'll get to our witnesses. We can't do any more taping of Dawson after he's arrested."

"There's no chance we're going to tape him again, anyway. Tonya Dawson is crazy now—naked in the moonlight crazy."

"An arrest starts the speedy-trial clock, Mark. If they held us to it, we'd have to take the case to trial in 70 days, maybe even less. There are other things we've got to get done first."

"Somebody's going to get killed. Somebody else is going to get killed, I mean."

The line was silent for a moment. Before Sally Thomas answered, she sighed deeply. "Yeah. Yeah, that's right. Let's do it. The case may get better as we go. I never thought I'd hear myself say that, but you're right, we can't just leave it alone, now. Can we do the warrant Monday?"

"I can wait till Monday. I'll see you there. When?"

"Nine o'clock okay with you?"

"See you at nine. Sally, will he have to know it's her?"

"No. I think we can write it up in a way that will keep her confidential—for a while, at least. But I can't guarantee we can keep him in jail pending trial. He might make bond. The drug thing is not exactly a capital offense."

"It's the best we can do, Sally. It's all we've got."

"I know."

"Sally, thanks."

"Mark."

"Yeah?"

"You can't arrest this guy by yourself."

"You tell me what else I'm going to do."

"I can get somebody to help you on a drug arrest. DEA or somebody."

"Fine with me."

"I'll have someone here Monday morning."

"Make sure it's somebody that's not crazy."

"I'll look around."

24

Varner and a DEA agent arrested Dawson early Monday afternoon. They stopped his truck on Poplar Ridge Road and cuffed him and put him into the back seat of the cruiser. The agent read Dawson his rights just as he got out of his truck. Dawson waited till the agent finished then said that he wanted a lawyer. He did not speak again during the entire trip to Charleston. Ten miles outside of town the dispatcher called Varner's number and told him to call Winter at headquarters from a public-service line.

The regional jail was only a couple of months old and was located off an exit from the Corridor just three miles south of Charleston. They led Dawson cuffed through the front entrance and to a booking window.

"You can make that call if you need to," the agent said to Varner. "I can take care of this."

Varner looked around the room for a phone. The agent pointed to a grey metal door across the room.

"Through that door. Just knock and badge them. There are phones in there."

Varner found the phone and punched up the number for headquarters. He asked for Winter.

"Mark, what did you guys do with the keys?" Winter asked.

"What keys?"

"To the truck. Dawson's truck."

"I think I got them. Let me look. Yeah, they're here. Why?"

"Truck's been wrecked. Somebody drove it off the road on Poplar Ridge and down the hillside. Hit a tree."

"Who did it?"

"Don't know."

"Where's Tonya?"

"That was my next question. Don't you know?"

"No. What's the wreck look like? Is there blood or anything?"

"Yeah. There was blood on the windshield. It was smeared blood right above the steering wheel. Truck's pretty tore up. They say it's totaled. Sampson found the truck."

"What was he doing there?"

"Nothin'. He was off duty. He's lookin' for her now, I 'm told."

ON HIS way back to Bandy, just before he left the Corridor, Varner hailed for Winter on the radio.

"He's in his office," said the dispatcher. "What do you need?"

"I want you to ask him something for me."

"Okay."

"Ask him if they found her."

"Okay. Give me just a few minutes."

Varner topped the next mountain and drove into the shadow of the highwall and pulled the cruiser onto the berm of the corridor and coasted out from behind the highwall and its shadow to where his view was open west and east. He looked right and far to the west and to the long ridge at the horizon which stretched from everlasting to everlasting like a floodwall of the gods. The sun was just touching the ridge and the level edge of the mountain broke the horizontal rays into visible streams and the light so prismed came across the lower hills and the valley like a spirit and lit the autumn trees with red and orange and gold and what lay before him in that moment before the shadows was an undulating crazy-quilt of glory.

"Charleston. You still copy me?"

"Yeah. I told you just a minute."

"I know. I know. I just wanted to know if I was still in range."

"They found her."

"Who found her?"

"I don't know. Winter says to call him when you get there. On the phone. That's all I got."

Varner looked at his watch.

"Tell him nine o'clock. I'll get him at home."

Varner drove fast on the narrow and winding roads between the Corridor and Bandy, as if trying to outrun the falling darkness. When he got to the barracks he stopped the cruiser with a slide on the cinders and ran to the door and unlocked it. Winter's wife answered the phone. "He's in the TV room." She said. "Let me get him."

"Mark?"

"Who found her?"

"Sampson found her."

"She hurt?"

"Yeah."

"How bad?"

"I'm not real sure. He took her to the hospital. Took her home first, though."

"Why?"

"To get clothes. She didn't have no clothes on when he found her."

"You know anything about the extent of her injuries?"

"I know where he took her. That tells me somethin'."

"Where?"

"Took her to Lightner."

"Mental hospital? In Kanawha City?"

"Yeah."

25

Lightner Clinic and Rehabilitation Center was a two-story brick building, painted white, that fronted on a four-lane highway. Before the road was built it had been the mansion house of a coal heiress. There was no sign on the building to identify it. Varner put the cruiser into one of the five parking spaces beside the house. As he walked to the narrow front porch, cars whizzed by so close to him that he could feel the breeze made by their passing.

At the reception desk, Varner asked the woman if he could see Tonya Dawson. He did not give his name or tell her that he was a policeman. It was very quiet in the room and the woman gazed at him over her glasses and then lifted a clipboard from her desk and looked it up and down, then looked at Varner again.

"Your name?"

"Mark Varner."

"Just a minute."

The woman stood and walked up a nearby stairway. In a few minutes she came back down. With her was a bulky man in a white uniform. The woman walked back toward the desk while the man in the uniform remained at the stair landing.

"I'm sorry. I'm not at liberty to disclose to you the identity of any patient, sir." She said.

"This is business, really." Varner said.

"I'm very sorry."

The woman sat back down behind the desk and opened a drawer and drew out what looked like a ledger and opened it and laid it on the desk-top. She took a pencil from a cup and appeared to focus on the page, her elbows on the pages of the ledger and holding the pencil with both her hands, the point in one, the eraser in the other.

"I need to speak to her. I can be very brief. Just a few minutes really. It's about a legal matter."

She did not look up.

"You may leave a number."

She cast a quick glance at the man in the uniform. He had not moved.

26

Varner entered Sally Thomas's office unannounced. The receptionist had been away from her desk and the door to the inner sanctum of the US Attorney's Office—a solid oak door with a passcard lock—was standing open, held back by a swivel chair. Varner, who was running a few minutes late and had left his badge inside his jacket pocket, walked through the open door and down the hallway.

She was at her desk and focused on some reading when he stuck his head through the doorway. The screen of her computer was busy with a pair of geometric forms which floated silently, constantly changing in color and dimension. Beside the open notebook on her desk in which she was quietly absorbed, stood a ceramic teacup. The cup was covered with a loose-fitting ceramic lid of the same floral pattern as the cup itself. Her office was full of things: boxes of documents, stacks of correspondence, transcripts, video-tape cassettes. The room carried the look not of dusty indolence, but of vigor. In it all a determined will to order was obvious.

She did not stand when he entered the room, but looked up from her reading and closed the notebook and stood it on a credenza. She showed no sign of being startled and she did not smile.

"Hi, Mark. Thanks for coming in. Leave that door open just a crack, please. There'll be traffic up and down that hall for the next hour."

He sat down in one of the two matching chairs before her desk and rested his right ankle on his left knee. "What's up? We got an arraignment? Bond hearing?"

"He was arraigned this morning. The bail hearing is set for tomorrow and they are coming after us. The UMW has already weighed in. Kyle Castle is representing Dawson."

"I don't know Kyle Castle. That name doesn't mean anything to me."

"It will. Castle represents the Union. They're screaming that we're taking sides in a labor dispute by making this arrest."

"We've got probable cause. That's all we need, isn't it?"

"Technically, legally, yes. But the timing is pretty obvious. If the judge thinks we were improperly motivated to make this arrest, he'll be much more sympathetic to defense arguments on any point. Castle has already talked to the press. They'll be lying in wait."

"I guess we knew that."

She sighed. "Strikes are strange animals around here. It's almost like a fight in high school or something. You just have to let them at each other. It's their business and anyone who gets in the way is...you know. It is so strange to me that I forget about it—how strong that feeling about it is. I can't say that I was really thinking of that when I authorized the arrest."

"We've got a strong case here, Sally. We've got threats on tape. The judge just about has to hold him, doesn't he? He's a danger to the community. That means pre-trial detention, doesn't it? How could it be any stronger? The judge can't let him go."

Thomas rested her elbows on the desktop and pressed her face into her open hands for a moment, then she sat upright again. She did not respond.

"What's the worst that can happen?" Varner asked. "If he makes bond, he'll have to be on good behavior. At least we'll have slowed them down."

"That's not the worst that can happen." Sally Thomas answered.

She swiveled her chair around to an open file cabinet behind her desk and lifted an expandable file out. She fished through the folders within the file and withdrew a document of several pages, stapled together. "Look at this," she said.

Varner uncrossed his legs, bent toward the desk and took the document. He rested his elbows on his thighs and held the document in both hands and scanned the first page and then looked up at her.

"I've got to ask you about this, Mark. Everything that's alleged in there. Do I need to bring in a witness?"

"A witness? What? You're going to read me my rights?"

"I don't like this any more than you do. But, there it is. A motion to dismiss based on outrageous government conduct. It's filed and we've got to deal with it. Don't think I've bought into it, Mark, but seduction of a witness is a serious allegation, and I've got to do this right. We've got to respond to them, and I need to know how—I mean whether—you can do that."

"What do you mean '*It's filed*?' Is this thing public?"

"No. Not right now. Castle filed it himself a couple of hours ago, right at the time the press was up there looking through the daily filings. He served me my copy by mail. I'll get it the day after tomorrow. One of our paralegals was up in the clerk's office when Castle filed this and she heard him joking about it. She got a copy and brought it to me. I ran to the judge's chambers and got it sealed before the press got to it."

She took the lid from the teacup and drank, then continued. "But it will become public. There will be a hearing and Judge Martin won't seal that."

"Martin got this case?"

"Yes. I had to get a Judge assigned to get the thing sealed. Martin got it."

"He knows me from another life. He's the guy who was a state judge before?"

"Yes. Till last year."

"He heard my divorce."

"Was that a contested divorce?"

"Not in the end, it wasn't. There was some preliminary stuff, though. She wanted to get the thing granted on grounds of adultery at first. For religious reasons. It all got worked out, finally. The lawyers...irreconcilable differences is easier for everybody. You know."

"How much did the judge actually hear?"

"He heard the whole thing. She just stood up in one of the early hearings and started on me. Crying and everything. It was out of order and he didn't consider it, officially, but he sure heard it. Pretty much the whole story."

"Was the story a true story?"

Varner did not respond immediately. He looked at his hands, then out the window. "Yeah. Everything that mattered about it was." He said.

"Think Martin will remember it?"

"I don't see how anybody could forget it."

"But he must've heard a thousand divorces."

"He'll remember."

Varner stood and stepped away from the desk and leaned against a tall file cabinet facing the desk.

"Sally, can he just do this? Is this legal? I mean, if we're going to charge somebody, we've got to get a warrant or an indictment or something. We've got to say mother-may-I. This guy just files a paper and all this stuff comes out in court. My wife will hear it. My parents. Her parents. It's not fair."

"No it's not fair, but they can do it. The legal theory is well established. Flip the page over. You see that case cite? Rochin v. California?"

Varner glanced out of the office window at the concrete and glass bank building across the street. Outside it was dark enough so that he could distinguish which rooms in that building had lights on. He turned the page and nodded at her.

"In that case a couple of cops were chasing a juvenile for drug possession. The kid outran the cops for a while and then stopped and swallowed the pills. All the kid had was a couple of pills. Without the pills, the police had no case, so they took the boy to the hospital and had his stomach pumped, recovered the pills and went after the kid. Supreme Court didn't like it."

"Nobody got their stomach pumped in this case."

"No, but the theory established in the case is broader than those specific facts. Other cases—with completely different facts—have been reversed under the theory. They're cited in there, too—at the very end. It's just a judicial outrage kind of thing. If the court thinks the police—or the government—went beyond the bounds of human decency to make a case, they can send us a message. Doesn't even have to be tied to a particular Amendment or Constitutional right. In this case they just say that you lured this pristine little wife of his into bed with you in order to make this case—a career case for you—and they say that that is outrageous. They say that that is why Tonya ended up in the mental hospital—because you led her on and then dumped her. I think they are setting it up to file a civil case against you if they win here. They filed an affidavit with this motion, her affidavit, and it's full of details. They say they have another witness to some of this. Pretty convincing on its face."

"So what do we do? What do we have to fight this with?"

"The truth, I hope. Do we have the truth on our side here, Mark? I've got to have a very straight answer here. If these allegations are true, then we run the risk of losing this case—a very real risk, I think—and you have to fight whatever other personal or career battles this might cause. But if you deny them and Castle shows up with pictures, then there's an obstruction of justice case to be made against you. I wouldn't be able to prosecute it because I'd be a witness against you. I want you to think about this, Mark. I'll let you review this affidavit before you answer me, if you want. Or, you can refuse to answer..."

Varner interrupted her. "My rights, I know. It's *not* true. There are things in it that are true. Things that will be hard to explain. But I did not seduce her. I never had sex with her. You can put me on the box. I know what happens if I'm lying. But I'm not lying. I've done wrong before, but not this time."

Sally Thomas took another drink of tea. She lifted the phone from the far edge of her desk and brought the receiver to her ear and punched a number.

"Mike, this is Sally. I'm going to be okay here this evening. No, that's all right. It's going to be okay. Thanks for sticking around."

She hung up the phone and took a new legal pad from a desk drawer and drew again the file from which she had taken the motion and took another document—this one much thicker—from that file.

"Here's the affidavit, she said. We've got to get through this thing, chapter and verse. I need to know where you were, where she got all this stuff, and who are the witnesses we can call to back you up against her. This is going to take a while."

27

Jack Sampson, in his 40 years, had been tired many times before, but he had never been tired like this. Even the worst exhaustions he had experienced had always had some echo of strength in them; even in combat where the combination of little food, no sleep, and the jungle's choking mixture of heat, humidity, and relentless insects had all worked to bring him panting, nose down, to the dirt, there had always been something left over—something down in the marrow of his massive bones that was resilient, that had already begun to replenish, that said, even if in a still, small voice, *I can take more. I can do it again. I will be stronger next time.* In fact, fatigue usually brought some comfort in that it made him conscious of the size and the potency of his body. When his limbs ached and throbbed, it was then that he was most aware of them, it was then he sensed most keenly that which onlookers noticed first—the awesome reserve of power within his frame. Of course, those feelings weren't as grand as they used to be. Age and abuse had taken some toll. These days, weariness was heavier and less pulsating than in the younger times.

But tonight all that was changed; tonight he did not feel heavy—he did not feel the now familiar weight of the years. Tonight he felt tired and emaciated—skin and bone, as if he had been starved, as if a light wind could carry him away. It was sickening to him and frightening too. He thought of the pictures of the starving Ethiopians. He felt himself drawn to the fetal position. His stomach began to ache. Why is there no escape, he thought. Why can't old things just go away and die? Doesn't God have a statute of limitations?

And now the still, small voice spoke once again. The words were strange to him but he was sure this was no false effect of delirium—this was a familiar voice, one that had never been wrong before. He did not question its authority and its words shook him to his soul. The voice said: "I cannot take any more. I cannot do it again. I will not—I will never—be stronger next time."

He killed the engine and stared into the river. The strike had closed the wash-plant four days ago and the stream once again ran crystal clear. He walked to the river. It was strewn with sycamore leaves, curled and brittle like cupped arthritic hands. He dropped his gun-belt onto the sandy bank, but otherwise was in full uniform as he waded into the stream. At knee-deep his calves began to ache with the cold. As the water neared his waist he drew a quick breath, but continued his wade without a pause.

At neck-deep he stopped, ducked under the water and began to swim upstream, toward the swinging bridge, his patent-leather uniform shoes making plunging "ka-thud" sounds with each stroke. As he reached the bridge he stopped and grasped a remnant of cable dangling from the middle pier. He held to it and floated downstream the length of the wire, then stopped in the current face up, like an anchored boat. He stared at the starry sky—the diamond sky—as the icy water swept around him. He held on till the cold needles pressing against his skin went blunt. Then numbness. Then, womb-like warmth.

Over ninety-nine per-cent of what flows through one river is exactly the same as that which flows through every other—water, that miraculous mixture of hydrogen and oxygen. The last one-hundredth of one per-cent is the stream's fingerprint. Every rock, every plant, every square foot of soil in the watershed adds its part to the mixture. Scientists can distinguish the water from one stream from the water from another, and so can a native. So can one who has grown up with a stream. And now Jack Sampson began to recognize so many familiar things: the slow, steady current, the last breath of the tomato plant odor from the ragweed and the horseweed that lined the river's banks. Then, those sweet hints of honeysuckle. He stared again at the midnight sky. The stars seemed to swirl as the sense left his body, their tiny lights blurring with his tears.

There, just down the stream, at the creek-mouth is R.L. Maddux and a little boy. R.L. and Jack. R.L. is wearing a miner's helmet; its beam points to a place in the weeds on the riverbank. Jack holds a gig. Its handle is a long piece of copper pipe, beaded with humidity from the midsummer night air. Jack slides his hand down the cool shaft, searching for a balance point. R.L. is still as a bird-dog, the light beam still fixed on the quarry. The boy lifts the spear in the direction of the light-beam. He stands one leg forward, like a tribesman, as he silently jabs the spear forward into the circle of light. He hears the familiar, hollow, wet gurgle of the frog being pierced.

Sampson, floating in the cold river makes a hollow, wet gurgle. He strained and buckled and twisted in the water. His vomit, like a ragged scab on the river's surface, was drawn long in the current and slowly pulled away. He looked down the stream again.

The old man and the boy are gone.

28

After some polite exchanges between the lawyers and the judge, all meaningless prologue to the anxious crowd, Kyle Castle stood and in his best choir voice announced his first witness. "Your honor, the defendant calls his wife, Tonya Dawson."

Sally Thomas looked back at the door, then leaned to the side and whispered to Varner, who sat next to her at counsel table. "I told you Castle knows how to dress a witness."

Tonya Dawson entered the courtroom from the rear door and walked to the witness stand at a bridesmaid's pace. She wore a calf-length corduroy jumper, navy blue, with a round collared, white cotton blouse, and an oversize pair of tortoise-shell glasses.

"I told you," Sally repeated, "a kindergarten teacher."

After being sworn, Tonya took the witness stand, crossing her ankles and folding her hands in her lap. She fixed her eyes on her husband.

"Tell us your name, please," Castle began.

The first series of questions allowed the witness to describe her home life with her husband. It was, according to the testimony, "very happy, except that Sam works very hard and has to be away from home too much." There were repeated questions about the couple's child whom, the witness established and re-established, was very sick and loved his daddy very much. That done, Castle lifted his legal pad from the podium and slowly approached the soft-spoken witness. His voice was reassuring, like a minister at a funeral. "Mrs. Dawson, do you know Corporal Mark Varner?"

Tonya Dawson dropped her eyes slightly. "Yes."

She said she had first met him when he came to her home one day last fall. It was just after her husband had left for work.

"He was wearing a gun," she said. "He told me he was with the government and that he needed to come in and talk to me. He said if I didn't talk to him there he would serve papers on me and take me in front of the grand jury. I asked him if he could come back when my husband was home. I was very scared and nervous. He said no he couldn't do that. He just needed to come in for a little bit. He said he didn't want to arrest me. I let him in then. My little boy was asleep and he has a condition. I didn't want to get arrested and have to leave my baby there by himself."

"What did Corporal Varner say to you when he entered your home?"

"Well," and now the tears came, "he told me that he knew Sam, my husband, had killed John Helton. He told me that he could prove that Sam had killed other people, too. He said the federal people had tapped our phone. He told me that Sam was going to go to jail and that I would probably go to jail, too." Her head was bobbing up and down with the vigorous sobs. She accepted a handkerchief from Castle. "He told me I would loose my baby."

Castle whirled around and glared at Varner as he walked back to counsel table. He poured a cup of water and carried it to the now flushed witness. "Did he ask you to do anything?"

"He said I could help myself by helping him. He said I could help him get evidence on Sam and then he would talk to the federal prosecutor and I would have a better chance of keeping my baby."

"Did you agree to help the officer, Mrs. Dawson?"

"Not at first. I told him I didn't know anything about any murder and I didn't see how I could help him."

"What did he say to you then, ma'am?"

"He asked me if I knew about Sam selling marijuana."

"Did you know about that?"

"Yes. I knew Sam sold it once in a while. I didn't like it, but there wasn't nothing I could do about it. We both used it till the baby came, then I started to hate it. I wanted to get away from it and our so-called friends who still messed with it. But Sam wouldn't give it up. He said it wasn't any different from alcohol. He got mad at me if I fussed about it too much."

"After you told Varner you knew about the marihuana, what did he say?"

"First, he told me that he had been recording me and that I had confessed to federal drug felonies, that I could go to jail for thirty years. He told me he could arrest me right then and there and take me to Charleston right then if he wanted to."

Sally Thomas looked up at Judge Martin. He was poker-faced and did not return the prosecutor's glance. Thomas continued to stare until she was sure the judge had seen her and was purposely ignoring her. Martin was a hard read; he practiced at being a hard read. But Thomas knew him, and she knew the judge was not amused.

"Did the corporal take you to Charleston, Mrs. Dawson? Did he arrest you?"

"No, oh no. I fell apart when he threatened me with that. I begged him please not to take me to jail, that I would do anything..."

"What did he say to you then, Mrs. Dawson?"

"He told me that helping him get evidence would take care of part of my problem, but I would have to help him other ways to get out of all my troubles."

"Did he say how else he wanted you to help him?"

"He said I could help him right then in the bed-room." The witness looked at Varner.

Did you have sex with Corporal Varner that morning, Mrs. Dawson?

"Yes."

"Why did you have sex with him, ma'am?"

"Because I was afraid he would take me away from my baby if I didn't. I was scared. I had nowhere to turn."

"How much education do you have, Mrs. Dawson?"

"Not very much. I quit in the tenth."

"Did you have a phone in your house, Mrs. Dawson?"

"Yes, I did."

"Did the officer ever tell you that it was okay for you to use it? That you could make a call or anything?"

"No, he didn't. He acted like he was in a big hurry, like we had to do this now or something terrible was going to happen."

"Did he ever tell you that you had the right to remain silent?"

"No."

"Did he ever tell you that you had the right to a lawyer?"

"No."

"What else happened that morning?"

"He told me that he knew Sam was going to go somewhere the next night to get paid for some marihuana he had sold. He told me he wanted me to go up with Sam and hide a tape recorder in my blouse and record the conversation."

"Did you do that, ma'am?"

"Yes, I did."

"Where did you go?"

"I don't know exactly where it was. It was somewhere in McDowell County, though."

"Whom did you see?"

"I don't know. I'd never seen the guy before in my life. I didn't really see him that good that night, either. It was dark."

"Did you record a conversation between Sam and the man he went to see?"

"Yes, I did."

"Is that conversation the same conversation which is recorded on this cassette marked as government exhibit number one? Castle held up a black cassette."

"Yes, that's it."

"What was that conversation about?"

"It was about marijuana. Sam told the man he wanted to be paid for the marijuana. Sam got real mad."

"Did you hear anything said about any murder?"

The witness shook her head in denial. "Absolutely nothing."

"When you made that tape did you believe that your husband killed John Helton?"

"No."

"Did you after you made the tape?"

"No. Well, for a while there I...I don't know...I was so confused for a while."

"Do you now believe that your husband killed John Helton?"

"No."

"Why did you make the tape?"

"I was scared to death. I knew people went to jail all the time for drugs. I thought I could go to jail. I thought that he..." the witness looked at Varner "would take me away from my baby."

"Would you have made this tape under any other circumstances?"

"No. I love my husband."

"Did you make another tape for Corporal Varner?"

"Yes."

"For the same reasons you made the first tape?"

"Yes."

"Did you have sex with Corporal Varner on other occasions?"

"Yes."

"Are you able to tell the court approximately how many times that happened?"

"About five."

"Where, ma'am?"

"Two other times in my house. Once in his police-car up on Joe's Creek when I was giving the first tape back to him. One time in the State Police barracks at Bandy."

"Why did you continue to have sex with Corporal Varner, ma'am?"

"At first I was just scared. Then it got to be a combination of things, I guess. I felt so bad. I was real confused. Sometimes he was real nice to me. He told me I just needed to change my life—to get away from my past with Sam. He told me he loved me. He told me he was going to leave his wife and marry me after Sam went to jail."

"Did you make any of these tapes of your own free will, ma'am?"

"No, he scared me. He lied to me and he used me." Here the witness went from an occasional sob to a full wail. "I can't believe the things I've done. I just don't know things. I didn't know about policemen."

Kyle Castle looked at the judge. He waited till Martin looked at him, then he shook his head from side to side, as if in disgust—as if to say, *What are decent people like you and me, judge, what are we going to do about this kind of thing?* After milking every second of drama out of the look of disgust, he said, "We have no further questions, your Honor."

Judge Martin looked over his glasses at Sally Thomas. "You may cross-examine." He said. Thomas could not read the judge's face. She began her examination in a monotone.

"Mrs. Dawson, you're lying about this whole affair, aren't you?" Thomas was standing now, but she had not left the counsel table yet and appeared to be occupied with a few loose papers she kept re-arranging on the table. She did not look at the witness. "Mrs. Dawson, you are lying about this whole thing, aren't you?" she repeated.

Tonya Dawson straightened a bit in the witness chair but did not raise her voice. "I have not lied about anything," she said.

"You've never had sex with this man, have you?" Thomas was still looking down at the table. She did not even look at Varner as she pointed an open hand toward him during the question.

"Yes, I have. I have had sex with him at least five times."

The prosecutor still did not raise her eyes from her papers. "The truth of the matter is, Mrs. Dawson, you wanted to have sex with him. You wanted to get him into bed. Didn't you?"

"That is a lie. No."

"And that is why you gave him the information on your husband, isn't it? Your husband beat you and you thought he would eventually kill you, didn't you?" Judge Martin began to glare at Thomas, who was still fussing with the papers, and still speaking in a monotone, as if she was reading assembly instructions for a wheelbarrow.

Tonya Dawson answered the question like a well-prepared witness, but there was no evidence that Thomas heard her answer. "That's a lie. I love my husband," she said.

"Mrs. Dawson, I suppose you are going to tell us that you had your clothes off during these alleged sexual acts, correct?"

Castle was out of his chair waiving his arms. "I object. This question, and questions like this one can serve no purpose but to further embarrass and humiliate Mrs. Dawson. It's harassment, your honor, nothing but harassment, and I object."

"What is the point of this, Ms Thomas?" Judge Martin insisted. "Why is it that you must know what clothes were on and what clothes were not?"

"Well, your honor, the witness has made certain factual allegations, very serious factual allegations. I am entitled to examine her in a manner to test her memory and perception of those purported events."

"I know the rules, Ms Thomas," the judge said. "If I must explain myself further, I mean this: what difference can it possibly make—a detail like this? And the court is disposed at this point to agree with Mr. Castle. This smells like harassment. What is your point?"

"Your honor, please. This is not harassment. I will make my point directly. I will only need a few more questions."

"Get with it then. And there had better be a point, counselor."

"Did you take your clothes off ma'am?"

"Of course," Tonya answered through quiet sobs.

"Did the corporal take his clothes off too, ma'am?"

"Yes."

"All his clothes, ma'am?"

"Yes."

"Every time ma'am?"

"Yes."

"There were five or six times, ma'am?"

"About that."

"Any of them during the day, ma'am?"

"What?"

"Did you have sex with the trooper during the daylight?"

"Yes," she shouted. "At least two of the times were in the middle of the day."

"I see. So, then, you had no trouble seeing what was going on then, correct?"

"Yes, Ms Thomas, I saw what was going on."

"No question about that, is there, Mrs. Dawson?"

"None at all, ma'am."

The prosecutor finally dropped the sheaf of papers. She walked away from the counsel table and halfway to the witness. She held out both hands toward the witness and stood motionless for an uncomfortable few seconds. She whispered the next question. "Then it is all a lie, Mrs. Dawson. It is all a contrivance. Because, if I were to tell you that Corporal Varner has two tell-tale markings on his body—two unmistakable features that one could only see when he is disrobed, you could not tell me what those are, could you?"

Tonya Dawson straightened her back. She smiled; not a kindergarten-teacher smile, but the smile of a predator before a kill. Her response was rapid-fire. "Yes, I do, ma'am. I'm familiar with those markings. He has an up-and-down scar just above his navel and a mole about the size of a quarter right in the middle of his back." She continued to smile.

Sally Thomas gulped audibly. She turned away from the witness and stared for a moment into the murmuring gallery, unfocused, as if amnesic. She walked back to counsel table; not to her chair—she stood in front of the table, between Varner and the judge. Facing Varner, she huddled down, waving her arms and directing accusatory whispers at Varner. Kyle Castle looked on with a satisfaction he could not contain; he chuckled as the frustrated prosecutor scrambled for a way out of the hole the witness had just put her in.

When Thomas turned back to the witness she was shaking her head slowly from side-to-side. She returned to the monotone. "You never saw those marks, did you, Mrs. Dawson? Somebody told you about them. Isn't that what really happened?" The delivery had completely changed. These were really questions, not statements. It seemed as if Thomas was truly searching for the answers; that she herself was unsure who to believe.

"No. I saw those marks. I had my hand on the mole, I touched the mole."

"Every time you had sex with him, ma'am?"

"Yeah." She nodded her head for emphasis in an assured, almost arrogant way, as a winning gunfighter might clap the dust from his hands.

Thomas threw up her open hands. "May I have a moment to confer, your honor? I think I am just about finished with this witness."

"Certainly, Ms Thomas. I assume then that you have already made the point which you earlier promised the court?"

"Yes, your honor." Thomas whispered as she again huddled around Varner. The conference lasted only a moment. "We have nothing further of this witness, your honor."

Kyle Castle stood up. "We rest, your honor."

"Does the government wish to present any evidence, Ms Thomas?" Judge Martin asked.

"Yes, your honor. The United States calls Jack Sampson. Patrolman Jack Sampson."

The courtroom was silent as the uniformed officer walked briskly to the stand. It was a silence born of curiosity. What did this patrolman have to do with anything?

The questioning of Sampson began at a quick, businesslike pace. It was obvious that both the prosecutor and the witness had been through this drill before. But Thomas's monotone had disappeared. The questions: "How long have you held the rank of patrolman?", were boring, but it was obvious that neither the witness nor the lawyer were bored. It was rote, but there was a snap—almost a nervousness—to the practiced dialogue. Faces in the gallery were focused, concentrated on the witness. Judge Martin was motionless, undistracted, with his head tilted slightly toward the witness.

"Do you know Tonya Dawson, Officer Sampson?"

"Yes, I have known her ever since she was a little girl—about twenty years. We live in the same town."

"What is her reputation in that town for truth-telling?"

With this question Kyle Castle, who had been resting his head in his hand, elbow on the counsel-table, relaxed into his chair. Negative character testimony was not going to cut it. It would not discredit the testimony of the girl who—much to his surprise and joy—could identify the markings on the trooper's body.

"That reputation is bad, ma'am. Very bad."

"And do you know Corporal Mark Varner of the West Virginia State Police?"

"Yes, I met him a couple of months ago when he was assigned to Boone County on a homicide investigation."

"Do you and the corporal get along well?"

"We have had our problems, ma'am."

"Have you ever been in a fight with Corporal Varner, sir?"

"Not a real fight. I punched him once during a basketball game."

"Were there spectators in attendance at that game?"

"A few. It isn't a big deal, but there are a few. Older policemen, some wives and kids, girlfriends."

"Did Tonya Dawson attend that game?"

"Yes, ma'am."

"How is it that you happen to recall that, officer?"

"I had a conversation with her right after the game. She had seen me hit Varner. She talked about it."

"What did she say?"

Kyle Castle was out of his chair as fast as if it had been set on fire. "I object, your honor. The question calls for hearsay."

The judge stared at Thomas with a look the prosecutor knew very well: his how do you answer that one look.

"Your honor, this is a hearing, not a trial. There's no jury here and the rules of evidence do not apply. This court knows how to weigh hearsay testimony."

"But your honor," Castle countered, "there is no need to spend the time it will take to go through the motions on this witness. She has called one cop to exonerate another. This guy will testify that Tonya Dawson told him something different than what she testified to here today. It's baloney, judge, and you don't have to let it come in. I object."

"The objection is overruled," the judge began slowly and calmly, "I'm going to let you ask the questions, Ms Thomas, out of an abundance of caution. These are very serious charges leveled against this officer. If they are proven, they will have implications for him far beyond the confines of this case. I will let you ask the questions, then, although I am not at all hopeful that this line of testimony will be meaningful. I must say, Ms Thomas, that your efforts to this point have been lost on this court and I have no idea why you believe this officer's testimony will be of any value."

Now the judge began to speed up and his voice rose as he continued. "As Mr. Castle observed, you are having one police officer vouch for another in the face of something all policemen fear: a charge of outrageous conduct. Is that it, Ms Thomas?" The judge did not pause for an answer. "Let me assure you that in deciding this case the court will take its own advice where the testimony of witnesses is contradictory. The court will look to the surrounding circumstances to determine which account is the more believable. Right now I have before me the testimony of a young woman who is able to describe with rather convincing detail the areas of this corporal's body which are normally hidden. It is also quite obvious to the court that this testimony came as a surprise to you. You may proceed."

"Thank you, your honor. Mr. Sampson, when Tonya Dawson spoke to you after the basketball game, what did she say?"

"She said she wanted to set Varner up. She said she hated him. He had been snooping around, and she wanted to set him up."

"By the way, Officer Sampson, where was Varner as you had this conversation with Tonya Dawson?"

"At the hospital, ma'am."

"How do you know that?"

"I saw them take him away, ma'am. He had been playing ball with us and they took him to the hospital from the gym."

"Why?"

"I had busted his face, ma'am. He was going to get stitches in the cut."

The prosecutor interrupted her own questioning as a young man in a gray pinstripe suit carried a cardboard box past the low wood railing dividing the well of the court from the gallery. The man, who had made his way through the courtroom without a sound, whispered to Thomas, who acknowledged with a nod. The man then set the cinderblock-sized box beneath Thomas's counsel table, and left as quickly and as silently as he had entered. Thomas looked back at the witness.

"You said that Tonya Dawson was going to set Varner up. How was she going to do that? How was she going to set him up?"

"She was going to cry rape. She wanted me to help her."

"Help her how?"

"She wanted to know about his body—what he looked like naked. She asked me if I had seen him in the locker room before the game. She wanted to be able to give convincing testimony."

"Had you seen Corporal Varner in the locker room before th e game?"

"Yes."

"What did you tell Tonya Dawson?"

"I told her that I hated him, too. I used some strong language. I told her that Varner had a scar just below his navel and a mole about the size of a quarter in the center of his back."

"You say you had just seen Varner?"

"Yes."

"Did you see any scar or mole?"

"No."

"Would you have seen such a scar or mole if any had been there?"

"Yes. I lied to her on purpose. I knew what I told her was not the truth."

"You lied to her on purpose, officer?"

"Yes, ma'am. Like I said, she told me what she was up to. I lied to her to protect Varner from these baseless charges that have been made in this hearing."

Kyle Castle was out of his chair, arms flailing like a choir director in overdrive. "I object. Object to the speech." His voice had lost its resonance. "Object to this witness's characterizations of the charges as baseless."

Judge Martin was at last amused. He fought his impulse to smile. "Is there a mole, Ms Thomas? What will be your evidence on this point? Is there a mole or a scar?" A faint collective snicker echoed in the gallery.

"No, your honor. Corporal Varner is prepared to exhibit his back and the area where the scar was supposed to be as well. Neither one is there, or ever has been, your honor."

"In light of that, Mr. Castle, why should your objection be sustained?"

Castle was caught off guard. He was still huddled with Sam Dawson at counsel table. "I'm sorry, your honor. The objection should be sustained because the testimony is irrelevant, it is conclusory and it is untrustworthy."

"Well, the trustworthiness issue would be disposed of by an inspection of the Corporal's back, would it not?" The judge raised his eyebrows.

"Well, I suppose, yes, it would, but…"

"And if the mole is not there, then the testimony would not only be conclusory, it would be fairly conclusive as well, it seems to me."

"No, your honor. I disagree. Such a showing would in no way be conclusive. In fact, we contend that the matter is absolutely irrelevant to the issue before the court."

"It does seem that the absence of any such mole might bear upon the credibility of Ms. Dawson. As I recall she testified…" Here the judge licked his thumb and leafed through a few pages of his notes. "Yes, I have it that she testified that she had her hand on this purported mole every time she…" Judge Martin looked up from his notes. "That was her testimony, wasn't it, Mr. Castle? Any dispute about that?"

"No, your honor. We do not dispute that that was the witness's testimony."

"And she was your witness; your only witness. It seems completely relevant to me, but I will withhold

ruling on the objection until Corporal Varner has testified. How much longer, Ms Thomas? Aren't we at a
point where we can wrap this up?"

"Yes, your honor. Just a few more questions. Officer
Sampson, do you recognize the man sitting next to me
at counsel table."

"Yes. That is Corporal Mark Varner of the West
Virginia State Police."

"Ever seen this man's back before?"

"Yes, ma'am. In the locker room before the ball game."

Thomas signaled to Varner who began to remove his
shirt.

"Officer, when Varner turns his back to you, tell us
whether or not you recognize it."

Sally Thomas turned to Varner and motioned for him
to turn his back to the witness and to the Judge.

"I do ma'am," Sampson answered.

"Corporal Varner, please display your back to the
court and to the defense," Thomas said.

Someone in the gallery could not hold a giggle as the
half-naked trooper backed up to the bench, then to the
defendant's table.

"Your honor, may the record reflect that the corporal's back has no mole on it?" Thomas asked. "I am prepared to photograph it and make the photo a part of the
record, but if we could reach agreement on the issue…"

"Any objection, Mr. Castle? Have you had sufficient
time to inspect the corporal's back?"

"Yes, we have, your honor, and no, we have no objection."

"Very well, then. The record will so reflect. Is there anything further, Ms Thomas?"

"No, your honor. The government rests."

"Mr. Castle?"

"May I have just a moment, your honor?" Castle was again huddled with Sam Dawson. Their dialogue was indecipherable, but quite animated, like a growling match between two dogs. At last Castle stood up. "We have nothing further."

"No cross examination?"

"No, your honor."

"Do you wish to make argument?"

"No, your honor. We believe the case is fairly before the court."

"Thank you very much, Mr. Castle. The court feels much the same way and the motion to dismiss is denied. The court finds that there is no credible evidence whatsoever of outrageous government conduct and is further persuaded of the truth of Officer Sampson's testimony that this whole charge was fabricated by Ms Dawson as a part of a scheme."

Now the Judge looked at Varner. He spoke slowly. ACorporal Varner, the court is very sorry for the embarrassment this matter has caused you. I know you understand that it is absolutely necessary for this court to take allegations of this kind very seriously at the outset. I also hope you have some appreciation for what Officer Sampson has done for you in this matter. Allegations such as those made here tend to have a tainting effect even when the court is not persuaded of their truth. However, I think you will have no such worry in this case. I have never seen a witness so thoroughly discredited."

The judge paused, then stacked his notes neatly, began to stand up, then turned back to his microphone. "Oh, yes. Trial in the case against Mr. Dawson will begin on Monday." Now the judge stood and stepped down from the bench.

"All rise. This court is now in recess," the clerk cried.

Sally Thomas sat back down in her chair at counsel table. She pulled a thin file folder from the box beneath the table and began reviewing it, page by page. She had closed the folder and pushed it to the back of the table before Kyle Castle approached.

"Okay. No mole. Nice trick, Thomas. I owe you one." Castle was smiling, but it was a forced smile.

The prosecutor rocked back on the rear legs of her chair. She did not smile. "Not my trick. It was Sampson's trick. Varner didn't even know about it till after you filed the motion."

"Good for Sampson, then. But I still don't get it— why Tonya Dawson would tell a cop about the scam she was going to pull on another cop, even if she did see him punch the guy. Stupid, I guess."

"Maybe not so much as you think. She had reason to believe she could trust Sampson."

Castle shrugged. "Oh, well. It's over now. What do you guys want from my man anyhow? He's looking at five max on this marijuana thing. Martin will never give him more than three, maybe less. He says he can help you with some other drug stuff in the county. What would that be worth to you? I'm looking for misdemeanors."

Thomas leaned forward, bringing the front chair legs back to the floor. She reached down into the cardboard box and lifted a black revolver in a clear plastic bag onto the table. The bag was sealed with a line of red tape marked EVIDENCE. "It's not going to be that simple for him, Kyle. We think your guy has some serious exposure on the Helton murder."

Castle took the packaged gun in his hand, looked at both sides, and shrugged confidently, like a boxer who has slipped a punch. "I've seen this thing before, Sally. I've also seen your ballistics reports, and never the twain shall meet. You're gonna have to do better than this to scare me. This gun means nothing. You kicked my ass with the mole story, but I won't be bluffed."

"Oh, but you have been," Sally Thomas said. "We had been, too. You haven't seen this gun before." Thomas again reached into the cardboard box beneath the table. Again she pulled a black revolver in a clear plastic baggie from the box. She laid the second handgun alongside the first on the counsel table. They were identical. Thomas held her hand beside the newly displayed gun as she spoke. "This is the gun you've seen, Kyle. We didn't have this other one till this morning. Well, that's not exactly true. Sampson got a pretty good look at it a few nights ago when Tonya was waiving it in his face. Uncomfortable for him at the time, but it made for great reading in the search warrant affidavit. While you were getting Tonya ready for her courtroom debut, and I must say it was a particularly impressive one for a while there, our guys were executing a search warrant on Sam and Tonya's happy home. No one was there this morning. Can you imagine that?"

The prosecutor lifted the second revolver from the table. "Found it under his pillow. Hasn't been printed yet. Seems like these searches always go so much smoother when there's nobody home."

Kyle Castle was unruffled. He lifted his hands in a *so what* gesture. "So my client has two guns," he said.

Sally Thomas shook her head side-to-side. "Not just two guns, Kyle. Two identical guns. Why?" The prosecutor continued. "This gun," she pointed, "is the one we got first. Tonya gave it to Varner six weeks ago. We had ATF do a records check. Sam Dawson bought it September twenty-first—the day after Helton was killed."

Sally waited several moments for a response, then began to replace the guns and paper into the cardboard box. Castle broke the silence. "I'll admit it's odd. But you know as well as I do that's a long shot from a case. You gonna offer anything on these drug charges in return for my guy's testimony or are we going to try this case?"

"Except for the ballistics, Kyle. We have done ballistics. That's the gun that killed Helton. The lab guy says it's a lead pipe cinch." Sally Thomas stood up and lifted the box with both hands. "I've had stronger evidence in a murder case before, but we've got a real decent shot now. A real decent circumstantial case with that ballistics report. Once we get the ball rolling like this, things usually get better for us. Tonya Dawson won't be a witness for us, it's true, but after that circus performance of hers today, she'll be worthless to you guys, too. Got another alibi witness, Kyle?"

"So there is evidence implicating my client…"

Here Thomas interrupted. She had been walking away from Castle and raised her voice to cut him off. "We've got a murder case, Kyle."

"Who is *we*, Sally? Since when did you guys get jurisdiction in murder cases? Your case—to the extent there is any case—is a state prosecution. Lacy Maze gets this one. I hate that myself, Sally. I hate to put my perfect record against him on the line again. You'd think after winning twelve acquittals in felony cases in a row Maze would have had enough of me. But, then, I guess I'm no different from anybody else. Lacy hasn't won a felony case in eight years. I just hate it. But, you know, I'm a professional, Sally. I'll do my job for my client no matter what it may cost me personally, no matter…"

Sally Thomas, who during this facetious harangue had turned in her tracks, now slammed the cardboard box onto the counsel table. She pulled a banded stack of light green, business-envelope-size cards out of the box and set them on the table, stopping him in mid-sentence. "There's more, Kyle." She continued taking these ragged stacks from the box and now slapped them down onto the glass-covered table.

"What's this?" asked Castle.

"These are ballots." The prosecutor pulled a top card from under the rubber band and read from it. "Local 612, May 10, 1984."

She pulled the top card from the next stack. "Local 1014, May 10, 1984". She pushed the cards back into their respective stacks. "These are ballots," she said. "Real ballots that were actually cast in the UMWA election here in Boone County in the spring of 1984. But these ballots were never counted. We found them in your man's closet during this morning's search. There are ten precincts, ten locals here, Kyle." Thomas passed her hand over the uneven stacks. "By our count of these ballots, Tagliani lost every local. By the official—the reported results, Tagliani won them all. These votes would have swung the election. These votes would have stopped the strike."

"So now we are talking about election fraud. Not exactly a new concept in West Virginia."

"Wrong again, Kyle. We're talking about labor racketeering. That *is* Federal, you know, and it includes murders carried out as a part of the racketeering activity. I get to keep the murder case this time and here's why: Sam Dawson killed John Helton, but it wasn't because of any drug deal. Dawson and Helton were conspirators in the 1984 election. They helped steal the election for Tagliana. They stole these ballots—with the help of a few others. We got these things the same place we got the other gun—in Dawson's bedroom during the search. Helton had kept them at his place till the night he was killed, that's why the place was ransacked. Dawson tore the place up trying to find these things."

"Sounds like a good theory, Sally. But it's just a theory. Who's going to be your witness to this big bad conspiracy? Helton? Or are you going to testify?"

"You can't get enough, can you, Kyle? Are you listening to me? We've got ourselves a witness, a fine witness. You met him today as a matter of fact. Sampson. He was in on the election conspiracy back in '84. He can give you the whole story, chapter and verse."

"That's a new twist. A police officer as a co-conspirator." Castle smirked. "There's a great opportunity for some cross-examination. 'Now, Mr. Sampson—excuse me—*Officer* Sampson, you had robbed ballots from a UMWA election before you took your oath of office to serve and protect the people of your podunk town—do I understand this correctly, sir? And sir—Officer—tell me again, please, why it is that you, being aware this election had been stolen, did not report this crime to the authorities till now?'"

"Oh, you can have some fun with him. You can have your usual fun with him. You can embarrass him and look like West Virginia's answer to Perry Mason till you're finished. Then the jury will go back to their little room and convict your client on every count in the indictment, including the murder. If you don't believe that, you are deluding yourself and you are ill-serving your client's best interests.

"You should wake up, plead him guilty, and cut your client's losses. The jury will believe Sampson. He doesn't have any deal—he doesn't benefit from his testimony at all. In fact, it's going to cost him his job. He gave it up because he couldn't live with himself any longer. He was trying to push Varner to get him to charge Dawson all along. When Maddux got killed, that was it. Maddux practically raised Sampson after his father was killed in the mines. Sampson couldn't live with his dirty secret anymore. You try to cross-examine that away."

Sally Thomas again started out of the room. This time she was moving more quickly. She did not look back at Castle, who was still seated on the prosecution's table as she spoke a final word. "I'll take a plea to murder one and let the racketeering stuff go if he comes in now and gives me the full story on the Maddux murder. If I'm guessing right, he's got enough exposure on that to get himself a shot at the Federal death penalty. Maddux fits the definition of a Federal witness in the statute, you know. Dawson probably never thought about that. Call me tomorrow or no deal."

"I'll talk with him in the morning," Castle said.

29

United States District Court for the Southern District
of West Virginia
AFFIDAVIT FOR SEARCH WARRANT
Comes now the affiant, Mark L. Varner and deposes
and says:

1. That in May of 1982 he graduated from the West
Virginia State Police Academy at Institute, West
Virginia and, upon such graduation, entered on duty as
a State Trooper with the West Virginia Department of
Public Safety, otherwise known as the West Virginia
State Police.

2. That he has continuously served in the West
Virginia State Police since that time, having attained the
rank of Corporal in August of 1989.

3. That in January of 1990, he was assigned to the
Bureau of Criminal Investigations of the West
Virginia State Police (hereinafter "BCI") as a plain-
clothes investigator.

4. That in March of 1992, in connection with his
assignment to a special Federal-State Law Enforcement

Task Force organized to investigate violence associated with the UMWA strike of the West Virginia coal-fields which strike began in August of 1991, he was deputized by the United States Marshal for the Southern District of West Virginia as a Special Deputy U. S. Marshal.

5. That in March of 1992, he was dispatched by BCI to the Boone County headquarters of the West Virginia State Police, located at Bandy, West Virginia, for the purpose of investigating the murder of John Helton, which murder apparently took place at or near Laurel Creek Hollow, in Boone County, West Virginia, on or about the 14th day of January, 1992.

6. In his capacity as a Special Deputy U. S. Marshal, he is authorized by law (Title 18 U.S. Code, Section 3124) to execute Federal Search and Arrest Warrants.

7. On the 2nd day of September, 1992, a woman identifying herself as Tonya Dawson and claiming to be the wife of Sam Dawson brought the affiant a Walton Martin revolver, .357 caliber, and informed the affiant that this gun was the weapon used by Sam Dawson to kill John Helton.

8. On the 2nd day of September, 1992, the affiant took that revolver to the West Virginia State Police Ballistics Lab where said revolver was test-fired and

examined according to standard scientific ballistics theory and practice and where bullets fired from that gun were compared to bullets and bullet fragments taken from the body of the deceased John Helton.

9. On the 2nd day of September, 1992, Technical Corporal Sandra Woods of the West Virginia State Police, who performed the ballistics and other examinations on that gun, told the affiant that that gun was very likely the same model and make of gun that was used to kill Helton, but was not in fact the murder weapon inasmuch as signature markings on the bullets fired from that gun did not match exactly with signature markings on those bullets removed from the decedent's body and further because, in Corporal Wood's opinion, and based on examinations performed on this gun before and after it was test-fired and which she believes to be reliable and which examinations have been long recognized and generally accepted in the field of firearms forensics, the gun given to the affiant by Tonya Dawson had never been fired before the test-firings were made on September 2nd in the ballistics lab.

10. On the 2nd day of September, 1992, the affiant returned from Charleston to Bandy, West Virginia and attempted to return the gun to Tonya Dawson. At that time he confronted her with the conclusion of the lab that the gun had never been fired before. Tonya Dawson

then said to the affiant that she knew that the gun had been fired before because her husband, Sam Dawson, had fired it at her. The affiant did not return that gun to Tonya Dawson, but rather kept the same in his custody.

11. On the 30th day of October, 1992, affiant traveled to Big Horse Creek Hollow in Boone County, West Virginia where he did surveillance on a double-wide mobile home known to him by observation and by hearsay from local citizens to be the residence of Sam and Tonya Dawson. At such place and time, and in the dark of evening, the affiant observed a man approach the Dawson residence from below. Upon his approach to the front stoop of the Dawson residence, the affiant heard three gunshots fired and saw the flash from those shots within the Dawson residence. After those shots, affiant saw the man who had approached the house run away from the house and back into the lower hollow from where he had come. Affiant came closer to the Dawson house and through the window observed Tonya Dawson holding in her hand a blue-steel revolver which appeared to be identical to the Smith and Wesson model 10 revolver which she had given to him earlier and which he had not returned to her.

12. The affiant knows through a search of city records and from other hearsay evidence from local citizens that Jackson L. Sampson ("Sampson") has served

continuously as a Bandy City police officer since May of 1979 and that he is a person with a good reputation for truth and veracity in the community of Bandy and the surrounding area.

13. On November 27th, 1992, the affiant had a conversation with Sampson in which Sampson related to the affiant the following information:

a. That on Oct. 30, he (Sampson) went to Big Horse Creek Hollow with the purpose of meeting with Tonya Dawson and convincing her to allow him to search for and take from her house certain documents which he believed were taken from the residence of John Helton on the night he was killed and which were the reason for his being murdered.

b. That as he approached the home of Tonya Dawson and as he came onto the front stoop of that house, Tonya Dawson opened the front door and fired three shots in his direction, all of which shots missed him.

c. That he believes that Tonya Dawson did not know at whom she shot inasmuch as he had not announced to her that he planned to come to her home that night, had not identified himself to her before the shots were fired and, further, inasmuch as the evening was dark and there were no lights on at the Dawson house as he approached it.

d. That on November 15, 1992, he accompanied Tonya Dawson to her home from the Lightner Clinic and Hospital from which she had been released after observation and treatment for symptoms he believes are associated with substance abuse.

e. That on November 15, 1992, Sam Dawson was not present in that home inasmuch as he had been and then remained detained on Federal drug charges made against him in a Complaint filed in the United State District Court for the Southern District of West Virginia on November 9, 1992.

f. That when he entered her house on that day, she asked him to take certain luggage to her bedroom closet and when he complied with this request, he observed on the floor of that closet and in plain view certain gray metal boxes bearing stenciled painted numbers identifying certain local UMWA union Locals which he recognized to be ballot boxes used by the UMWA in its 1988 presidential election in Boone County.

g. That he participated in that UMWA election as president of Local #1257 and as an official poll watcher in Boone County, West Virginia and there and then saw that certain gray metal ballot boxes were surreptitiously and wrongfully removed, after the polls were closed, by John Helton and Sam Dawson and others working with them for the benefit of Timothy Tagliani in his effort to win election as National President of the UMWA, and which boxes were taken away and hidden and replaced by those workers with identical boxes which contained fake ballots the great majority of which had been marked by those same men and their agents and confederates on behalf of the candidate Tagliani, all for the fraudulent and unlawful purpose of increasing the probability that Tagliani would be elected national president.

h. That he verily believes that, inasmuch as Sam Dawson has remained incarcerated since the day he (Sampson) observed the boxes in the closet, those boxes are still present in that closet and the same are and contain evidence of criminal conduct, to wit: mail and wire fraud and tampering with a UMWA election, all in violation of Federal Criminal law.

14. Further this affiant saith not.

Epilogue: Sampson

Jack Sampson walked out of the Federal building. The sky was pigeon grey and patches of dirty snow hid in loamy depressions between the bushes lining the sidewalk. But Sampson did not notice the sky, the snow, or the dirt. He did not think about the months that lay immediately ahead—the inevitable appearances on the witness stand, the humiliation of cross-examination, the change in the way the people in the county would talk to him. He did not think about how he would earn a living.

He was thinking of none of these things as he slowed his stride to match a sensed meter—the cadence of a dream.

Epilogue: Varner

Varner came back into the courtroom and sat on the front pew of the gallery. There was no one else in the courtroom and the lights in the high ceiling had been dimmed. It was very quiet. He stared at the judge's bench and leaned against the back of the pew and relaxed his shoulders and rested his forearms on his thighs. He sat there for a long time.

A rear door opened and Varner turned his head and looked across the long room and saw a security guard in a blue blazer standing in the doorway. The door opened into the bright hallway and the guard held open the door and in his other hand he held a walkie-talkie. He looked back into the hallway and spoke to Dana Varner. She did not look into the courtroom and she did not see Mark. The guard nodded his head slowly at Dana and said that this judge was a smart man and nobody got much past him. Dana agreed and looked away from the guard and down the hallway and called to Varner's son whom Varner could not see.

The guard was an older man and he continued to hold open the door and to smile at Dana.

She was an ordinary girl and Varner looked at her and saw things he had never seen before and he gave thanks for his ordinary life. He thought of a favorite song, an old love song, and he thought of those things that hold this world together.